HOME OF THE BRAVE

#6

HOME OF THE BRAVE

LOREN LONG & PHIL BILDNER

SIMON & SCHUSTER BOOKS FOR YOUNG READERS

NEW YORK   LONDON   TORONTO   SYDNEY

SIMON & SCHUSTER BOOKS FOR YOUNG READERS
An imprint of Simon & Schuster Children's Publishing Division
1230 Avenue of the Americas, New York, New York 10020
This book is a work of fiction. Any references to historical events,
real people, or real locales are used fictitiously. Other names, characters,
places, and incidents are products of the author's imagination,
and any resemblance to actual events or locales or persons,
living or dead, is entirely coincidental.
SIMON & SCHUSTER BOOKS FOR YOUNG READERS is a trademark
of Simon & Schuster, Inc.
For information about special discounts for bulk purchases,
please contact Simon & Schuster Special Sales at 1-866-506-1949
or business@simonandschuster.com.
The Simon & Schuster Speakers Bureau can bring authors to
your live event. For more information or to book an event, contact the
Simon & Schuster Speakers Bureau at 1-866-248-3049
or visit our website at www.simonspeakers.com.
Book design by Tom Daly
Hand Lettering by Mark Simonson
The text for this book is set in Century 731 BT.
The illustrations for this book are rendered in charcoal.
Manufactured in the United States of America
0310 FFG
2 4 6 8 10 9 7 5 3 1
Library of Congress Cataloging-in-Publication Data
Long, Loren.
Home of the brave / Loren Long and Phil Bildner. — 1st ed.
p. cm. — (Sluggers ; [6])
This is the sixth book in the Sluggers series (previously published as
Barnstormers).
Summary: Having suffered great losses in New Orleans, the
Payne family returns to their Baltimore home, where they
have a final showdown with the Chancellor's men.
ISBN 978-1-4169-1868-4 (hardcover)
[1. Baseball—Fiction. 2. Supernatural—Fiction. 3. Brothers and sisters—
Fiction.] I. Bildner, Phil. II. Title.
PZ7.L8555Hom 2010
[Fic]—dc22
2009043142
ISBN 978-1-4424-0612-4 (eBook)

To Jennifer Flannery,
the magical one from the outfield,
and
Kevin Lewis, survivor
of the Cultural Revolution, and the
last man standing, always.
—P. B.

To my father,
William G. Long,
who introduced me
to the Big Red Machine.
I'd still rather go to a ball game
with you than anyone.
—L. L.

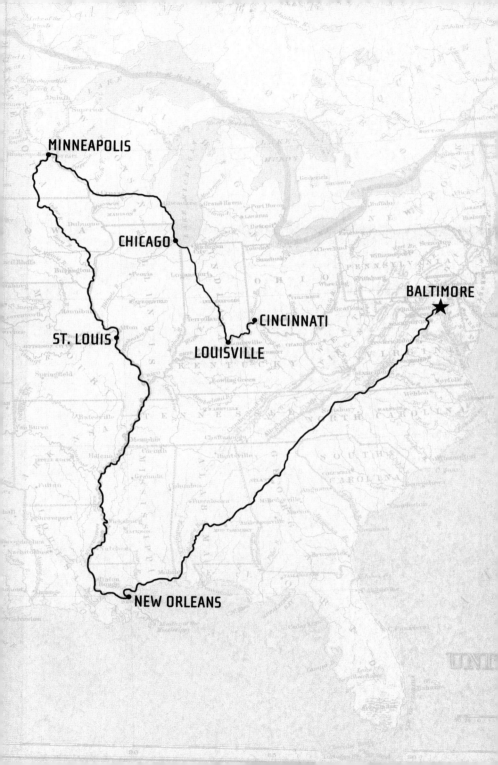

MINNEAPOLIS

CHICAGO

CINCINNATI

ST. LOUIS

LOUISVILLE

BALTIMORE

NEW ORLEANS

HOME OF THE BRAVE

Pregame Recap for
HOME OF THE BRAVE

★

From city to city, the Travelin' Nine have struck a chord with crowds and played like champions. The Chancellor may have plucked some strings to cancel the St. Louis game, but the mysterious old man joined their band and revealed his identity: He is the Chancellor's father. Maybe he can finally help the Payne kids gain an upper hand in their game of cat and mouse.

But in New Orleans, there were still plenty of sour notes. Elizabeth was exposed as a woman and forced into a skills competition, which she handily won. And Griffith finally uncovered the mole: Crazy Feet, who leaves the team heartbroken—not to mention short a player. Graham, however, steps in to face the famous Cy Young and—with the help of a little magic—leads the barnstormers to another victory.

But even the magic baseball has its limits. As the team packs for the next leg of their journey, the Chancellor's men attack Uncle Owen and the children. Uncle Owen is shot and the kids can barely hear him as he whispers something that could change everything. Are the Travelin' Nine ready for their final inning?

★

Contents

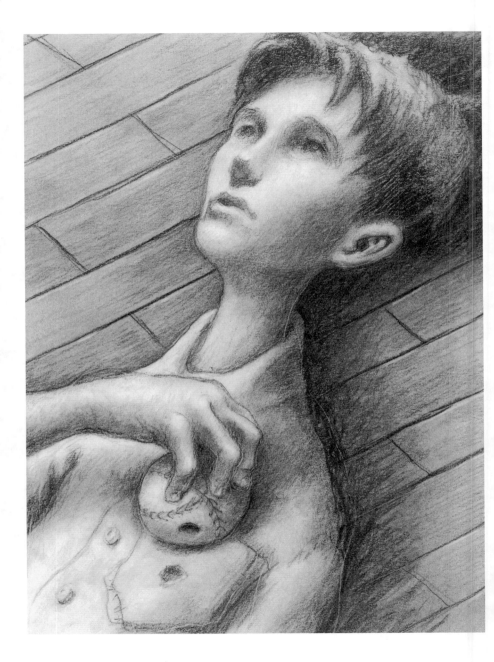

"They shot you!"

PROLOGUE

★

The Attack and the Aftermath

 **uddenly the door** to Uncle Owen's room burst open. Three of the Chancellor's men stormed in. One brandished a gun.

Truman leaped to his feet.

Woof!

The ferocious bark sounded more like a lion's roar. Every hair on the hound's back stood on end.

"No!" Ruby screamed.

Graham! Griffith didn't plan his actions; there wasn't any time. He leaped in front of his brother, yelling, "Get out!" faster than he could blink.

"Give us the baseball!" one of the goons shouted at Ruby. He kicked the bedroom door shut.

The two other dark-suited men were hollering as well, but Griffith paid no mind to their words. The only thing that mattered was that they were heading straight for him. Griffith raised his fists. Barreling over Uncle Owen, one of the goons lunged at Griffith. But before he could reach him, Truman leaped like a rabid dog and sank his teeth into the intruder's leg.

Bang!

A shot rang out.

The Chancellor's thug punched Truman's snout. As the hound loosened his grip, the goon kicked him away. Truman hit the wall by the bed, toppling the lamp on the end table and dislodging the mirror.

Yelp! Yelp!

Griffith wanted to race over to Truman, but he couldn't, not with the other goon reaching for Ruby and Graham. So he dove at that thug.

Bang! Bang!

Wrapping his arms around the thug's frame and using every ounce of strength he had (and some he didn't know he had), Griffith *lifted* the goon off the ground and rammed him into the wall next to the door.

Bang! Bang! Bang!

Griffith and the thug crashed to the floor as the gunshots echoed in the small room. Shielding his head with his arms and shutting his eyes, Griffith couldn't tell if more shots were being fired or if the same bullets were ricocheting off the walls.

"No!" Ruby shrieked.

"Griff!" Graham screamed.

Even though he could hear his brother and sister's cries, Griffith didn't respond. He could feel the thug moving next to him, and if he reacted to their calls, he had no idea what the goon might do.

And there was a second reason why Griffith remained absolutely still: the piercing pain above his heart. It felt as if he'd been stabbed with the end of one of the flaming bats from Chicago. He'd been shot. Griffith fought panic.

"No!" Ruby screamed again.

Stay calm. Don't move.

The Rough Riders must have heard the commotion, Griffith told himself. Happy's house was big, but not *that* big. They'd arrive any moment.

Griffith felt a rush of air. The door had been opened, and the thugs by the entrance were shouting—arguing. However, Griffith couldn't focus on their words, only on the burning below his neck. Was he bleeding? Did the goons think he was dead? Were they about to check to see if he was breathing?

His mind accelerated. Where exactly were

Ruby and Graham? Was Truman okay? What about Uncle Owen? As he thought about the others, the pain in his chest seemed to subside. Or was he simply distracted? Griffith wanted to open his eyes, but didn't yet dare.

Stay calm. Don't move. Not until they're gone.

The thugs were arguing about the baseball now. "There's no time!" cried one. "They're going to discover us any second!"

The next thing Griffith heard was the sound of disappearing footsteps, followed by scampering across the floor.

"Griff!" Graham was shaking his shoulder. "Wake up!"

"Say something!" Ruby was squeezing his fingers.

Griffith squeezed back.

"Griff!" Ruby screamed. "You're alive!"

For the first time since the attack, Griffith released the tension from his face. He managed a small smile.

"I think so," he whispered, opening his eyes.

"Where are you hurt?" asked Graham. "They shot you!"

"I think not," he replied. Without lifting his head, he placed a hand on his chest. Then he reached into his shirt pocket—which now had a hole in the front—and pulled out the baseball.

"The baseball saved you!" Ruby exclaimed, taking it from her brother. "The baseball stopped the bullet!"

"I think so," he whispered again.

Griffith grimaced as he sat up. Even though the baseball had protected him, he was still in some pain from the struggle with the Chancellor's goon, as well as from the force of the bullet hitting the ball.

His anxious eyes searched for Truman—and found him. The old hound stood near the remains of the lamp and shattered mirror. His tail began to wag the moment the boy looked his way. A surge of relief charged through Griffith. Truman hadn't been shot either, but as the loyal dog hobbled across the floor, it was clear he'd been badly bruised. When Truman reached Griffith, the hound's tickly tongue licked his cheek and chin.

"There's still only one hole in the ball," Graham said, taking the sphere from Ruby and examining it. "Wait a sec!" His eyes popped. "The new bullet entered the *same* hole!"

Griffith, Ruby, and Truman leaned in. The fresh bullet had indeed followed the identical path as the one that had been blazed a year ago in Cuba.

"The baseball saved my life," Griffith said, wincing. His chest burned with each breath. "Just like it saved Uncle Owen's."

Uncle Owen.

All three whirled. He was hidden from view by his tipped-over wheelchair.

"Uncle O!" shouted Graham. He passed

the baseball back to Griffith and speed-crawled across the bedroom floor.

Ruby tailed close behind.

"Uncle O!" Graham shook him like he'd shaken his brother moments ago, though not nearly as hard. "Say something."

Uncle Owen didn't respond.

"No," Ruby sobbed. "Wake up."

Griffith tried to hurry after his brother and sister, but the residual pain in his chest wouldn't allow it. As he gingerly made his way across the room, he heard the sound of footsteps again, though they still weren't close.

When he reached Uncle Owen, Griffith gasped. There was blood everywhere, all over his shirt and pooling around his head. His eyes were closed. He wasn't moving.

"You can't die, Uncle Owen," Griffith said. "You can't."

Then Uncle Owen's right arm moved. Ever so slowly, he began to raise it in Ruby's direction. She leaned in, and his searching fingers found first her face, then her necklace, tracing its metal links until they reached the keys.

Uncle Owen's lips were moving, but no sounds were coming out.

"What is it, Uncle O?" Graham asked.

Griffith glanced at Truman. The hound's ears were on end, but instead of facing Uncle Owen, he was staring at the door.

The three Payne siblings inched forward. Uncle Owen gasped several times before uttering:

"Tell Guy . . . tell Guy I had to. Tell him . . . I'm sorry."

The door to Uncle Owen's room swung open. But it wasn't Woody or Scribe or any of the Rough Riders bursting in. Rather, it was one of the Chancellor's goons, the one Griffith had tackled.

Griffith spun around and moved to dive in front of his brother and sister. The sharp pain in his chest stopped him. Griffith's eyes met Truman's. Struggling to his paws, the injured hound tried to block the thug's path, but the dark-suited man easily swatted the dog aside.

However, instead of heading for Graham or Ruby, the thug charged at Griffith, barreling into him. The goon slammed Griffith's head into the floorboards and ripped the baseball from his hand. Scrambling to his feet, he shoved Ruby and Graham aside and then elbowed Truman in the neck. But instead of racing back into the hall—where more approaching footsteps could be heard—he ran full speed toward the large bedroom window.

Shattered glass flew about.

The Chancellor's man was gone. And so was the baseball.

1

★

In Ruby's Words

Uncle Owen is dead.

It's taken me four days to write those four words. But I still haven't said them out loud. Neither have Griff or Graham. Because once we do, it becomes real.

It is real.

Everything has changed. Again.

It's amazing how quickly everything can change. It's scary. So scary.

<u>Uncle Owen's last words</u>

"Tell Guy . . . tell Guy I had to. Tell him . . . I'm sorry."

What did he mean?

What was he sorry for?

How can we possibly tell Dad anything?
Why did he speak in the present tense?

Griff thinks Uncle Owen was confused.
Maybe that's what happens when you're
taking your final breaths. Uncle Owen
was probably still thinking about the
childhood memory he had just shared.
That's why he said what he did.
I don't know what to think. I only
know we'll never know for sure.

Today is Thursday, September 7. We're
on our way to Baltimore for the funeral.
Right now, we're somewhere in Mississippi
or Alabama. After a month on the road,
we're heading home.
The games in Charleston and Atlanta
and everywhere else the Travelin' Nine
were supposed to play have been
postponed. Luckily, the teams in those

other cities have been understanding. I guess they really want to play against the Rough Riders. They don't mind if it has to be a week or two later than originally planned.

The "Investigation"

The police kept us in New Orleans for four days. They wouldn't let us leave during their investigation. Finally they told us their findings were "inconclusive."

We don't need an investigation to tell us what happened. We know:

Uncle Owen was murdered.

Looking at those words in my journal makes me want to scream. They killed Uncle Owen on purpose. I know they shouted something about how they weren't supposed to shoot anyone, but I don't believe that. Not at all. When you have guns, you shoot things. If you

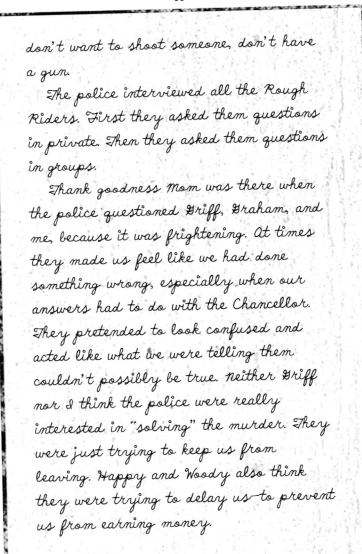

don't want to shoot someone, don't have a gun.

The police interviewed all the Rough Riders. First they asked them questions in private. Then they asked them questions in groups.

Thank goodness Mom was there when the police questioned Griff, Graham, and me, because it was frightening. At times they made us feel like we had done something wrong, especially when our answers had to do with the Chancellor. They pretended to look confused and acted like what we were telling them couldn't possibly be true. Neither Griff nor I think the police were really interested in "solving" the murder. They were just trying to keep us from leaving. Happy and Woody also think they were trying to delay us—to prevent us from earning money.

$$$$$$

We must have the $10,000 by the end of the month, but we are running out of time. I'm no longer certain it's possible for us to raise the money by the deadline.

In New Orleans, we earned more than $1,000. We didn't make that much money in all the previous cities put together. With more than $1,900 in total, everyone was filled with optimism as we packed for Charleston, Atlanta, and elsewhere. But then . . .

We need a miracle.

Funerals

I hate funerals. Before this summer, I'd never been to one. Neither had Griff or Graham. Now we're attending our second in two months.

At least there isn't a third funeral. That's what I keep telling myself. Our baseball saved Griff, just like it saved Uncle Owen during the war.

But it couldn't save Uncle Owen a second time.

And now we no longer have the baseball. The Chancellor does.

It's scary how quickly everything can change. So, so scary.

2

★

Planning Ahead

still can't believe the base-ball is gone," Ruby said, holding her head.

"No one can," said Graham. He peered across the baggage car at Griffith, sitting against the far wall. "Aren't you going to say anything?"

When Ruby had said they needed a private and safe place to discuss everything, Griffith had suggested the baggage car. However, their mother wouldn't allow it. Not at first. Since the attack, she'd insisted that at least two adults accompany them wherever they went. The grown-ups even slept in the same room with them. Only after Scribe had surveyed the compartment, the Professor and Tales escorted them there, and Woody promised to stand guard by the lone entrance did she reluctantly agree to give the kids some time to themselves.

"What do you want me to say?" Griffith finally answered. He looked at Ruby, lying against an oversize canvas duffel several feet from Graham. "The Chancellor has our baseball. What else is there to say?"

"We have to figure out what to do about it," Ruby replied, putting her hand into her empty pocket and frowning.

"Right now," said Griffith, "there's nothing we *can* do." He couldn't mask his frustration.

Ruby sat up. "I'm afraid of what *he* can do with it," she said.

"Do you think the Chancellor has powers now that he has the baseball?" Graham asked, looking from Ruby to Griffith.

Neither replied. It was the question no one wanted to ask, let alone answer. But Graham had dared to. What if the Chancellor was able to use the baseball just like the kids could?

Griffith turned away. Resting his hands on Truman's head, which was propped against his thigh, he peered around the luggage compartment. Suitcases and duffels filled the shelves that lined three of the walls. The baggage shifted with the rocking train, and Griffith wondered if the worn-out leather straps securing the travel bags would hold them in place for the entire the trip. Extra luggage was strewn about the floor, but there was still plenty of room for the three Paynes and Truman to maneuver.

"If he does have powers," Ruby said after a few moments, "we won't just sit by and let him use them against the Rough Riders."

Her tone was defiant. "We'll be able to see the magic on the field, and then we'll find a way to deal with it."

"We'll do the same thing we always do," said Graham. "We'll stand together, think positively, and figure things out." He clenched his fists. "Ruby's right. We're not just giving up."

Griffith managed a small smile. Seeing his sister and brother bristle with fire and optimism made him proud, but as much as he wanted to share their hope, he couldn't. Without the baseball, he felt helpless, and after talking with some of the Travelin' Nine in New Orleans, he knew they felt that way too. Preacher Wil and Doc weren't even certain the Chancellor still had the ball in his possession. They thought he might have put it someplace where no one else could get to it.

"We should talk to Josiah," Griffith whispered. "If anyone has answers, he does."

"He's so sad," Ruby said. "Every time I look at him, I want to cry. It's terrible."

Josiah had barely spoken since Uncle Owen's death. Whenever any of the Rough Riders tried to talk with him, he responded with one-word answers, nods, or shakes of the head. Most of the time he stood off by himself, staring into space and mumbling. None of the barnstormers knew how to reach him. How do you console someone whose only son sends out men with guns to threaten others? How do you comfort a person whose offspring is partially responsible for a murder?

BARNSTORMERS: *team that tours an area playing exhibition games for moneymaking entertainment.*

"Preacher Wil's been trying to talk to him," Griffith said. Truman's floppy ears perked up at the sound of his owner's name.

"I'll never forget the look on Preacher Wil's face when he first saw Truman after the shooting," said Graham.

"Me neither," Ruby agreed.

When Preacher Wil had arrived in Uncle

Owen's bedroom, Truman was crumpled on the floor in a pool of blood. Without a doubt, Preacher Wil thought the hound had been shot dead, and instead of racing over, he'd staggered backward. He even let out a soft yelp that sounded like Truman crying in pain. After realizing that the dog had only been injured, Preacher Wil could barely contain his joy. Tending to the hound's wounds, he looked at Truman with pride—the canine had been injured trying to protect the kids. In the face of great danger, he'd been fierce and fearless.

But days later, Truman still hadn't fully recovered. He was constantly licking the scrapes and cuts on his neck and belly, and he was not yet able to put weight on his left front paw. Preacher Wil thought Truman may have broken a bone or two in the leg, and that the old hound's limp might be permanent.

"I can't get over Woody," Griffith said softly.

"What do you mean?" Graham asked. He stood up.

"He's taking Crazy Feet's betrayal the hardest."

Upon learning that Crazy Feet was the Chancellor's mole, the Rough Riders had been devastated. None of the war heroes could comprehend one of their own turning on them. Now whenever Crazy Feet came up in conversation, the soldiers' faces turned solemn. Except for Woody's, which became lost. When he heard Crazy Feet's name or anything related to him, Woody excused himself and walked away.

"I need to tell you something," Graham said, plopping down next to Griffith. He then waved Ruby over. "It's about what happened in Minneapolis."

"What made you think of it now?" asked Ruby. She sat in front of her brothers.

"Woody," Graham replied. He stared at

Griffith. "He told you all about what happened in Cuba, and one of the things . . . one of the things reminded me of something that happened during the game in Minneapolis."

"What are you talking about?" Griffith asked.

Graham glanced at Ruby and then looked back at his brother. "It's about what Woody said . . . what Woody said about time standing still in Cuba." Graham swallowed. "During the game in Minneapolis, that happened to me. Time stood still."

"Tell us." Ruby leaned in.

Graham placed a hand on Truman's back. "Everything stopped. Right in the middle of one of Preacher Wil's pitches. All the players and cranks just froze. And it was dead silent. No clapping, no cheering, nothing. Even the snow hung in the air. I was the only thing moving. I could touch people, eat their

CRANKS: *fans, usually the hometown fans. Also called "rooters" (see page 157).*

24

". . . that happened to me. Time stood still."

food, and . . . and drop snowballs on them."
Graham looked from Griffith to Ruby. Both
stared, wide-eyed; Ruby gripped her necklace. "I headed onto the pitch"—Graham's
words quickened—"and out to right garden
because St. Anthony Falls had appeared
behind Woody, and the water was frozen
and crystal clear, but I was still able to pass
through without getting a single drop on
me." Graham paused. "Then I saw Dad. I'm
sure he was—"

PITCH:
*playing field.
Also called
"green oasis"
(see page 157).*

RIGHT GARDEN:
*right field. The
outfield was once
known as the
garden. So left
field was referred
to as "left
garden" and
center field was
called "center
garden."*

"Hold on," Griffith said, shaking his head.
"You had me up till now, little brother. But
that's impossible, and—"

"No, Griff. He was there. On the river.
Once I passed through the waterfalls, I was
standing on the edge of the Mississippi, and
Dad was down there on a raft. He called out
to me. He said, 'Happy birthday!'" Graham
placed a hand on his chest. He could feel his
heart beating. "I chased after him as fast as

I could. It was so real, the realest dream I'd ever had, but I knew it couldn't be happening and—and—Dad disappeared before I could reach him."

Graham stared at his brother and sister. For a long moment they sat in silence. The only sounds in the baggage car were the rattling of the shifting luggage and the rhythmic clicking of the train's wheels rolling over the railroad ties. His story was hard to believe, but after all they'd been through, it was harder *not* to believe.

"There has to be a connection," Griffith finally said.

Ruby nodded. "It's too similar for there not to be."

"What do you think it means?" Graham asked.

"It could mean anything," replied Griffith. "Maybe . . . maybe when time stopped in Cuba, death did too. That's why Dad was able to save lives. And then in Minneapolis, maybe something else stopped, and that's how he was able to wish you happy birthday in your dream."

"I don't understand," Graham said.

Griffith shrugged. "I'm just thinking out loud and trying to make sense of it." He stroked Truman's injured paw. "But Dad's dead."

"If Dad were alive," said Ruby, "I don't think I'd . . ." She didn't finish the thought.

Graham stood up, hurdled a wicker storage trunk, and walked across the compartment. He was so relieved to have finally told Griffith and Ruby about the dream or vision or encounter or whatever it was. Pressing his face against the side of the car and gazing through a knot in the wood, he tried to catch a glimpse of the passing scenery, but since it was almost nightfall, he couldn't see much of anything.

"It's more than a coincidence," Griffith said.

"I wish you had told us sooner," added Ruby.

Graham turned around. "You wouldn't have believed me."

"We could've asked Uncle Owen about it," Griffith said.

All three fell silent again, though this time only for a few seconds.

"I can't believe he's gone," Ruby whispered.

"Dad and Uncle Owen," Griffith said, frowning.

"At least we know where they are." Graham shuffled back over and sat down in the same spot. "In heaven."

Griffith leaned forward and kissed Truman on the top of the head. Then he reached out for his brother's hand. "More than at any other time, we need to be together. The Chancellor has our baseball.

He's more dangerous and unpredictable than ever."

"But everything's not lost, Griff," Ruby said, placing her hand atop her brothers'. "Like Dad used to say, in baseball and in life, anything's possible."

Graham pumped his fist. "It ain't over till it's over."

3

★

Eyes All Over

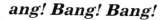**ang! Bang! Bang!**
The loud knocking on
the door to the sleeping
compartment jolted the
three Payne kids awake. Elizabeth and
Bubbles, both of whom had been sleeping on
the floor, sat up and tensed. Truman stood
tall, the hair all along his back on end.

Bang! Bang! Bang!

"Wake up!" Woody called. "Get your
things. I reckon we need to get off."

Bubbles leaped to his feet and slid open
the door. Woody ducked in.

"We're in Atlanta," he announced. "But we're gettin' off and hidin' out for the day." He closed the door. "They know we're headin' to Baltimore. They may know we're on this train."

"What time is it?" Graham asked, rubbing an eye with his palm.

"Almost dawn."

"How could they have found us?" Ruby wondered. She tossed her blanket to the floor and hopped off the bed.

Woody rolled his broad shoulders. "Ruby, I reckon there are eyes all over."

"Did the police tip the Chancellor off?" Griffith stepped into his boots.

"Could've been the police," Woody answered, opening the door and peeking into the hallway. "Could've been anyone. Railroad employees, conductors, restaurant workers, other passengers. Who knows?"

"Eyes all over," Graham repeated.

"He may not be here in person," said Woody, "but he's with us."

The barnstormers walked swiftly and quietly down the narrow aisles toward the back of the train. Even though the sun's early morning rays were streaming through the windows, the passengers in the rear cars were still sleeping. If any awoke, surely they would've been suspicious of such a large group filing through.

"Two more to go," Happy said as they crossed between cars. "We need to get to the second-to-last car. We'll exit from there."

"It feels like we're on a military mission," Tales added.

"Well, if this is what a military mission feels like," Graham said with a grin, "war must be fun."

"No, Graham," said Scribe sternly. He rested a hand on Graham's shoulder and wagged his forearm-sized finger in front of the youngest Payne's no-longer-smiling face. "There's nothing fun about war. War happens when all else fails."

"Scribe's right," Tales added. "I said this felt like a mission only because these are desperate times, and we are out of options."

The barnstormers reached the second-to-last car and squeezed into the entranceway at the far end, away from where the passengers were sleeping.

"When the train stops," Happy explained to the group, huddled close in the cramped quarters, "we're not going to use the designated exit. The passengers scheduled to disembark will use the doors at the front of the train. The conductor is allowing us to use this auxiliary egress, but we need to be discreet."

"Once on the platform, we must try to blend in with the others already at the station," Josiah added. "Our destination is the building by the ticket office."

"How do we know it's safe?" Griffith braced himself against the side of the shimmying car.

"The eagle, Mr. Griffith," Josiah replied.

"He told us about the Chancellor?" asked Griffith.

"That is correct, Mr. Griffith. He flew ahead. Alerted me of the danger."

"Are the Chancellor's men in this station?" Ruby asked.

"Very possibly, Miss Ruby." Josiah pinched the bridge of his wire-rimmed glasses. "Which is why we must exit with extreme caution. We will head to Baltimore on a different, later train. That will help ensure our safety."

Rounding a gentle curve, the train began to slow. The chuffing of the laboring engine came at longer intervals. The screech and grind of the wheels grew so loud that both Elizabeth and Graham covered their ears.

"We're almost there," Happy addressed the group again. "We'll disembark in small groups on that side." He pointed to the door behind Bubbles and Preacher Wil. "Walk swiftly, but don't run. Like Josiah said, we want to blend in. If all goes as planned— which it will—it will simply look like passengers are exiting from the front and back of the train."

"But we're not all getting off," the Professor noted.

Elizabeth gasped. "We're splitting up?"

"Doc is remaining onboard," the Professor replied.

"Why?" Elizabeth asked. "What if they find him?"

"They won't," said Doc. "They'll never recognize me."

Everyone turned.

Griffith's jaw dropped as he caught sight of the thin, clean-shaven man walking toward them. "Doc?"

None of the barnstormers had realized the Travelin' Nine's third bag man hadn't been with them as they made their way to the back of the train.

"Didn't recognize me, did you?" Doc rubbed his beard-free chin.

"You look so different!" Ruby exclaimed.

"Which is why I'll be fine." He looked around at the others. "I'm still heading to Baltimore. By the time you arrive on Sunday, the funeral will already be arranged." Doc's eyes settled on Elizabeth. "But only with your permission. Would that be all right with you?"

Elizabeth nodded once. "That would be very kind."

"The fliers will be made, and the match will be coordinated as well," Doc added. He

THIRD BAG MAN: *third baseman. The first baseman was often called "first bag man" and the second baseman was often called "second bag man."*

MATCH: *baseball game or contest.*

"Didn't recognize me, did you?"

lifted a sheet of paper from his breast pocket. "Happy, the Professor, and Josiah have provided me with a list that will more than keep me busy!"

Suddenly the train lurched forward, then back. The engine stopped chuffing, the wheels stopped screeching, and the brakes hissed.

"It's time." Josiah pointed out the open door at the ticket office across the platform, where the eagle sat perched high atop the steeple.

"Who's going first?" Graham asked.

"Scribe, Tales, and Josiah," Happy replied, his voice stern. "I've already made the groupings." He waited for the three men to gather by the exit. "Walk one behind the other," Happy instructed. "As if you're strangers."

"I'll take up the rear once the three of us are off," Scribe said, his tone equally stern. "So I can keep an eye on them."

Happy glanced at the list in his hand. "Graham, Woody, and Elizabeth will go next. You three will pretend you're a family. I suggest you hold hands. We'll watch you from the train. Scribe and the others will watch you from across the platform."

"Should I hold my mother's hand or Woody's?" Graham asked.

"Both," answered Elizabeth. "You'll stand between us."

Griffith swallowed. His arms and legs tingled. Were they walking into an ambush? Were the Chancellor's men awaiting their arrival in the station? Griffith gazed anxiously at his brother.

"Once they reach the ticket office," Happy continued, "the Professor and Bubbles will accompany Griffith and Ruby. Then the rest of us will follow."

"I'll walk with Truman," Preacher Wil said. "We'll travel like we always do."

Happy nodded, then looked to the group. "Four minutes from now, we'll all be safely at the building next to the ticket office." He pointed the first trio to the exit.

Scribe hopped off. He walked several yards down the platform, picked up a pair of milk crates, and placed them by the exit. The crates looked nothing like the rolling steps for the passengers at the front of the train, but no one in the depot appeared to notice. With an outstretched arm, Scribe guided Tales and Josiah down the makeshift stairs.

As the three headed across the station, Griffith stepped to the edge. "Keep your eyes open," he whispered to Ruby.

"Do you think they're here?" she asked.

"No, I don't."

Despite his words of assurance, Griffith couldn't help thinking of what Woody had said: *Eyes all over.* Still, he felt he should ease his sister's worries.

Watching the first group traverse the station, Griffith could feel his heart beating. It would be pumping even harder when it was Graham's turn. And then his. He scanned the station. There were others milling about, but since it was early, the depot wasn't crowded. If anyone approached Josiah, Tales, and Scribe, the barnstormers would be able to provide them with ample warning.

But no one did.

"Next group," Happy announced matter-of-factly, when the first trio neared the ticket office.

Elizabeth looked to Griffith and Ruby. Then she took Graham's hand and squeezed.

"You don't let go of me," she said.

"I promise," Graham replied.

"Or me," said Woody.

Hand-in-hand-in-hand, the three headed down the crates and out onto the platform.

Shielding his eyes from the sun peeking

between the brick buildings and tall trees beyond the station, Griffith watched his mother, brother, and Woody cross the platform. On his left, he could feel Ruby inching closer, her long hair brushing against his arm. Griffith tapped his pursed lips with a clenched fist. The three looked like a family—exactly as they were supposed to. Griffith could hear his mother talking and Woody laughing, a laugh Griffith had grown so familiar with on the train from Minnesota. . . .

Suddenly a person burst onto the platform. Ruby grabbed Griffith's hand. But it was just a small girl racing to see an adult.

Then another person charged out. Griffith held his breath. But once again it was a child, this time a young boy selling the morning newspaper.

"Our turn," the Professor said, waving Griffith and Ruby forward.

"You two ready?" asked Bubbles.

Griffith let out a long breath and looked at Preacher Wil and Truman. The hound seemed to nod. Again. Griffith smiled, for at that moment, he knew they were all going to make it safely across the station.

In a front of the doorway to the building by the ticket office, the barnstormers gathered around Happy.

"Less than four minutes," he declared, checking his timepiece. "Quicker than planned. Well done, troops."

Graham stood at attention and saluted him.

Happy smiled. "But we're not out of the woods. We still need to stay close and keep our eyes open. As we head over to the hospital where we'll be staying, let's try not to draw attention. Let's—"

He stopped. Josiah was pointing across the depot.

The train was preparing to leave. A station attendant had just wheeled the stairs away from the front car. But a quartet of dark-suited men was now racing across the platform and ordering the worker to roll the steps back to the train. The four men barged by the conductor and boarded right as the locomotive's whistle sounded and the wheels began to turn.

Griffith ran a hand through his hair. The goons thought they were still on the train. The Chancellor *did* have eyes all over. But thanks to the eagle, they had outsmarted the Chancellor.

For now.

4

★

Protecting Graham

ven though the barn-stormers spent a full day in Atlanta, they didn't see any of the city. Instead they stayed at Fort McPherson the entire time.

Following their service in Cuba, both Professor Lance and Uncle Owen, like many other soldiers wounded in action, were sent to Fort McPherson, which doubled as a hospital. A year later the army base remained a medical center, and some of the doctors and nurses who had treated the Rough Riders were still on staff. Using their military credentials and his connections, the Professor was able to secure rooms and food for the team.

"Today we rest," Happy said after the Professor had assigned everyone to their quarters. "Catch up on your shut-eye. Our train to Baltimore leaves at first light."

Like good soldiers, the group heeded Happy's orders. The barnstormers spent most of Friday sleeping, breaking only for meals and a midafternoon tour of the grounds.

At dawn the team headed back to the station. There was no sign of the Chancellor's men, and the eagle didn't provide any warnings. Nevertheless, Elizabeth insisted that, like the day before, they try to blend in while crossing the platform. Ruby and Griffith held hands with Scribe. Woody walked arm-in-arm

Elizabeth insisted . . . they try to blend in while crossing the platform.

with Elizabeth, while Graham followed close behind, accompanying his "grandpa" Harry, who ambled slowly to the train.

Onboard, the barnstormers settled in before gathering for breakfast. Then, after the meal, Happy reserved the dining car for a team meeting.

"When we're in Baltimore," the Professor addressed the group, "Graham will be flanked by at least two of us at all times. No matter where we are." He then motioned to Griffith, seated at the table beside his mother, and to Ruby, her face buried in her journal on the bench next to Scribe. "Depending on the circumstances, one or two of us will be assigned to each of you as well."

"Two," said Elizabeth flatly.

"Two," Graham agreed. "We can't be too careful."

Griffith looked at his brother, sitting on the floor at the Professor's feet. Graham had turned eight less than two weeks ago, but the events of the last couple of months had aged him way beyond his years. Prior to this summer, his brother had been a carefree child, oblivious to the world around him. But no longer. Graham understood so much more. Griffith started to smile. The others had to see his brother's growth too. How could they not? But then Griffith thought about the words he'd shared with Graham and Ruby so many times on this journey:

See the things that other don't.

He glanced at Truman. For a change, the hound wasn't sitting with his head in Griffith's lap. He was with Preacher Wil, who was massaging his injured paw. Even though the attack had taken place days ago, Truman was still hobbling. Yet not once had the dog whined or whimpered. Griffith smiled again. The hound really did possess all the qualities and traits "true men" aspire to have.

"When it comes to promoting the match," the Professor went on, leaning against a counter with three large coffee urns, "we'll need to choose the spot wisely."

"I'll take care of that," Elizabeth said. "I've spent most of my life in Baltimore. I know where the people go."

"The eagle will guide us too, Mrs. Elizabeth," Josiah added. "Not only must we find the best place, we must also find the safest."

"Safety first," said Graham.

He gazed across at Ruby, his eyes landing on her empty pocket. They no longer had *his* baseball. Peering around the dining car, he studied the faces. Graham saw how everyone looked at him, checked on him, protected him. He hadn't always been aware of it, but he was now. And he understood why. So much—everything—rested with him.

Graham wasn't going to let anyone down.

"The same goes for practice," the Professor continued. "We'll need to locate a safe field."

"I know of several we can choose from," said Elizabeth. She turned to Josiah. "Can the eagle scout those as well?"

"Of course, Mrs. Elizabeth," he replied.

"I reckon since we're talkin' 'bout playin' ball," Woody pointed out, "let's save us some time and figure out the batting order."

HURLER: *pitcher.*

Professor Lance nodded. "Not a bad idea." He pivoted to Preacher Wil. "Are you still comfortable hitting in the eighth spot?"

"I am," the Travelin' Nine's hurler answered.

"I'm still comfortable hitting last," said Elizabeth.

"And I'm comfortablest hitting leadoff," Graham declared, beaming.

Griffith laughed. "That's not even a word." He picked up a stray sugar cube from the floor and flung it at his brother.

Graham ducked out of the way. "It is now!"

Understanding his extra burden didn't mean Graham had to stop having fun. And it certainly didn't mean he had to stop joking around with Griffith.

"I say we stick with our New Orleans lineup," Graham said. "It worked there, and it's going to work here."

Woody smiled. "I reckon I like the boy's confidence," he said. "If it ain't broke, why fix it?"

I don't feel like talking this afternoon. I haven't said a single word at this meeting. neither has Scribe, sitting next to me. We're both just writing in our journals. I've tried peeking at what he's written, but each time he's caught me, tilted his journal, and wagged his quill.

I don't have to read what he's written to know what—who—he's writing about:

Uncle Owen. Everyone's thinking about Uncle Owen's funeral.

No one wants to talk about the funeral, and I understand why. It hurts too much. Once it's brought up, nothing else gets accomplished. Everyone becomes too sad.

Like me.

Looking up from her journal, Ruby stared across the dining car at her eight-year-old brother. She dipped her hand into her empty pocket. The tips of her fingers found a thread. She lifted it out. It was from their baseball. In an instant, Ruby felt her eyes begin to water. She slipped the lone string back into her pocket.

They *needed* the baseball.

5

★

Home to Baltimore

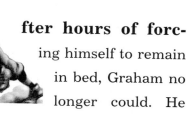

fter hours of forc-ing himself to remain in bed, Graham no longer could. He simply wasn't going to fall asleep. Pulling back the covers, he slid off his bunk and, so as not to disturb his brother and sister, tiptoed across the compartment. He unhitched the locks on the door and turned the knob.

Scribe and Tales greeted him the moment he stepped out. The two Rough Riders had been assigned the night shift and were guarding the room. Graham knew they would never let him go for a walk, so he joined the soldiers seated on the corridor floor. He opted to remain quiet, though; he didn't want to distract the duo while they were on watch.

Dangling his hands between his knees, Graham lowered his head. Ever since this afternoon's meeting, his mind had been racing, and the pinballing thoughts weren't easing up. He was going to have to be the hero. He was going to have to stop the Chancellor. In the end, everything was up to him.

SECOND SACK MAN: *second baseman. The first baseman was often called "first sack man" and the third baseman was often called "third sack man."*

Graham peeked over at Tales. The second sack man fought to stay awake, his head bobbing against his shoulder. Then Graham looked at Scribe, buried in his journal like he'd been during the meeting. Was that what they thought too? Did they also think it was all up to Graham? Was that what they *knew*?

• • •

"There's Camden Station!" Graham exclaimed, leaning out the window and pointing up the tracks.

"You sound like you've never seen it before," Ruby said, rolling her eyes.

Griffith glanced back at his sister. "Of course we've seen it, but we've never ridden into it on a train."

Ruby shook her head. She refused to join her brothers as they gawked and gaped at the enormous brick passenger terminal. She simply couldn't get excited about a railroad station she'd been to many times. Whenever relatives or friends visited from out of town, they always arrived on the Baltimore and Ohio Railroad, and the family would gather in the station and wait for their guests. A couple of times their father had taken them to the terminal just so they could see the modern trains, like the one they'd transferred onto a short time ago back in Washington, DC.

Because they had to switch trains, the barnstormers had awoken early, but no one seemed to mind. Everyone wanted to catch a glimpse of the historic buildings, especially Preacher Wil and Josiah, who'd never been to the nation's capital. Pulling into the District of Columbia, they saw the U.S. Capitol building, as well as the Washington Monument, the tallest structure in the United States.

Now Graham said, "I don't see Doc yet," and he leaned so far out that Griffith grabbed his brother's belt loop. Graham looked back. "Don't worry, Griff, I'm not going to fall."

"I know you're not," he replied, "because I'm not letting go!"

"Doc's probably waiting on the other side of the platform," Elizabeth said, joining her children. "They only let ticketed passengers by the tracks." She motioned to the end of the car, where the rest of the Travelin' Nine had gathered. "Let's go stand by the exit."

Taking Graham by the hand, Elizabeth led her children down the narrow aisle to where Josiah was addressing the ballists.

"The station should be safe," he said. "The eagle hasn't indicated that there is any danger. Nevertheless, we should proceed with caution and without delay."

"We don't have to split up this time?" asked Ruby.

The Professor shook his head. "No, we can walk together." He pivoted to Bubbles, Woody, and Preacher Wil. "You three are on Graham duty."

BALLISTS: players.

"Yes, sir," Bubbles said, saluting the Professor like he would a ranking officer.

Preacher Wil pointed Truman to Griffith. The hound hobbled over.

"I'll take good care of him," Griffith said, scratching behind the dog's ears.

"You always do." Preacher Wil stroked

his chin and then waved Graham over, but Elizabeth didn't let go of his hand.

"Before we leave the train," she said to her children, "I need for the three of you to listen closely." She waited for them to look up. "These next couple days are going to be difficult. Don't take it for granted that you're going to be able to handle this funeral. That's not how funerals work. They are never easy, and you don't ever get used to them." She draped her arm around Ruby and drew her nearer. "Your uncle was a special man. It may not seem like it right now, but he was. He was an amazing source of strength and support."

"He was a great man," Ruby said softly.

Elizabeth nodded. "He had his flaws, but he was a wonderful human being. He will live forever in our hearts."

"Just like Dad," said Graham.

"Just like your father," Elizabeth whispered.

"Are you four ready?" Woody asked, stepping over.

"We are," Griffith answered, standing up tall and wiping the corner of his eye with his shirtsleeve.

"Grammy, you stay between Bubbles, Preacher Wil, and me," Woody instructed. Then he pointed to Griffith and Ruby. "And you two pick an adult to walk with."

As a team, the barnstormers exited the train. But once on the platform, there was no sign of Doc. Nor could they find him anywhere in the station. So they headed out onto Camden Street.

Walking up the block, Griffith was struck by how foggy it was for so late in the morning. It made it difficult to spot faces. He couldn't ever recall a summer day quite like this one in Baltimore. The weather reminded him of the morning he, Woody, and Truman had returned to Minneapolis and found Josiah

Through the mist, a familiar figure began to emerge.

waiting by the university dorms. Glancing around, he wondered if the steam from the trains was contributing to . . .

Griffith stopped dead. Through the mist, a familiar figure began to emerge. He looked so different without a beard, which, along with the low clouds, was the reason Griffith hadn't spotted him right away. Tendrils of fog seemed to cling to the man, even as the haze faded and revealed his identity.

Guy Payne.

6

★

The Greatest Shock of All

ad!" **Graham shouted.**

Before any of the Rough Riders could prevent him from racing off, Graham was charging down the block. Griffith and Ruby followed close behind.

"Dad!" Ruby cried.

Up the street, Guy Payne ran as fast as he could toward his family.

Graham was first to reach his father, leaping into his arms. Ruby grabbed him around the waist, while Griffith hugged his father over his sister. Guy Payne corralled his children, kissing them repeatedly on the tops of their heads.

"You're safe!" Guy declared.

"You're alive!" Graham yelled into his father's ear.

Guy stiffened. His eyebrows nearly reached his receding hairline.

"You came back!" Graham exclaimed.

"Of course I came back," he replied, flinching.

Graham squeezed his father. "I knew you'd come back. I just knew it."

Guy stared at his stunned wife, who stood a few feet away. Even though he didn't understand his family's reaction, tears of happiness flowed down both cheeks. His hands refused to let go of his children.

The Rough Riders were just as shocked by the reunion. Scribe and Bubbles stood with mouths agape, unable to utter a single syllable. Tales tugged so hard on one end of his bushy mustache that some of the hairs came off in his fingers. Woody beat his bow-legs to the point that his knees buckled. And the Professor gave the cord of his eye patch such a yank that it snapped, and he had to retie it.

Elizabeth wobbled as she gazed at the *impossible* sight of her husband standing before her. Her shaking hands covered her mouth and nose. Tears streamed from her eyes too.

"We sure weren't expectin' to see you," Woody said, the first Rough Rider to speak.

Confused, Guy shook his head once and plunged into his explanation.

"For days I've been searching for leads on your whereabouts," Guy said, still holding tight to his offspring. "It's been difficult because I've had to stay out of sight. It's made me frantic." He looked over at the terminal. "I

started checking all the stations in the city—
Mount Royal, President Street, here. I was
hoping to find one of Happy's railroad bud-
dies, anyone who could tell me anything."
He nodded to the old-timer. "Finally I found
someone who'd heard you might be arriving
this weekend."

"So where've you been?" asked Griffith.

Guy motioned across the street. "In that
building over there. I was—"

"No," Ruby interrupted. "Not the last few
days, the last few weeks."

"The last two months," Griffith clarified.
He placed a hand on his father's shoulder.
"Where have—"

Smack!

Elizabeth slapped her husband across the
face.

"How could you do this to us?" she blurted,
her voice quivering. "How could you do this
to your own family?"

Guy's puzzled expression turned to one of anguish. "Do what, Liz?"

"We thought you were dead." Ruby clutched her father as tightly as she had the moment she'd grabbed on.

"Dead? What made you think I was dead?"

"The boating accident," Graham answered.

"What accident?"

"Dad, there was a funeral," added Griffith.

Guy released his grasp and grabbed his head. "A funeral?"

"We thought you were dead," Ruby repeated.

Guy lowered a trembling hand to his mouth and covered his gasp. Searching the eyes of the Rough Riders, he realized that all the soldiers had believed he was dead too.

"A funeral?" Guy said again. He spoke through his still-shaking fingers. "For—for me? That doesn't make sense. I escaped from—that wasn't what we planned."

"Planned?" Elizabeth's eyes narrowed. "What do you mean planned?"

But Guy didn't have a chance to answer.

"We must go!"

Everyone turned. An out-of-breath Doc was charging toward them.

"We must go!" he repeated, panting. "It's not safe here. The thugs will be—" Doc stopped midsentence, grabbed his chest, and teetered. Scribe caught him before he toppled. "I believe I'm seeing a ghost," Doc uttered.

Guy shook his head and forced a pained smile. "I'm no apparition," he said. "I'm alive and real."

"You are," Elizabeth whispered, the edge fading from her tone. She touched the cheek she had slapped a moment ago and ran the back of her fingers across her husband's clean-shaven chin. Then she straightened his tie.

"I'm sure there's a reasonable explanation for this," Doc continued, getting his wind back, "but there's no time now. We must leave." He pointed toward Howard Street. "His men came through twice yesterday. They will return. They've been in Baltimore since I arrived, but they haven't recognized me. That will change when they see everyone." He turned to Happy. "I've arranged for transportation to an inn by the harbor. We'll stay there temporarily until—"

"I've made other arrangements," Guy interrupted. "We're splitting up."

"I reckon it may be safer if we stay together," said Woody. "Ever since the Chancellor—"

"Please, Woody," Guy cut him off too. "Baltimore is my home, my city. I'm asking you to trust me."

Woody smiled. "Guy Payne, I could never stop trusting you."

"I second that," the Professor added.

"Huzzah!" several of the Rough Riders chimed in.

Guy Payne bowed his head. "Thank you."

"So what's the plan?" Doc pressed, scratching his chin where his beard used to be and glancing anxiously up the street. "We're not safe here."

"Take the Rough Riders back to our house." Guy spoke to Doc. "You know where that is, yes?"

Doc smiled. "The inn at the harbor was merely a stopover, a decoy to throw the Chancellor's goons off our scent. Your house was our final destination."

"Use whatever transportation you arranged," said Guy. "Or you can use the horses I've—"

"We're taking the horses!" Happy declared with a raised fist. "The Rough Riders belong on horseback."

"HUZZAH!": *common cheer to show appreciation for a team's effort.*

71

Doc grinned. "But what about Preacher Wil?" He motioned to the member of the Travelin' Nine whom Guy had yet to meet.

"I can ride," Preacher Wil said, tipping his cap to the Payne family patriarch. A formal introduction would take place later under less hurried circumstances.

"What about Josiah and Truman?" the Professor asked. "The dog can't ride, and he's too injured to run."

"Josiah," Guy said, greeting the old man with a single nod and a tap of the temple. Then Guy smiled at the hound. "They'll come with me. As will my family." He faced his three children again. "But we won't be riding horseback. We'll head to my furniture warehouse Underground Railroad–style, hiding in the back of a carriage."

"That's how we went to Happy's in New Orleans," said Graham. "Uncle Owen had us ride in a wagon under a tarp with all these crates of fruit—"

"Where is Owen?" Guy asked. There was an edge to his voice.

The Rough Riders fell silent. As one, they looked to Elizabeth; her expression turned somber.

Stepping to her husband, Elizabeth raised her hand to his face and placed it gently against his cheek.

A single tear fell from Guy Payne's eye, rolling across his wife's fingers.

"I'm so sorry, Guy." Elizabeth wiped the corner of his eye with a knuckle. "He's gone."

"You kept me alive."

7

★

What Really Happened

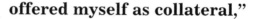

offered myself as collateral,"
Guy said. "I gave myself to the
Chancellor."

In the hayloft of the barn adja-
cent to the furniture warehouse behind his
office, Guy Payne huddled with his family,
Josiah, and Truman, whom Guy had carried
up. His three children sat cross-legged in
front of him, Graham so close that his knee
brushed against his father's pant leg.

"I didn't fake my own death," Guy said,
resting his hand on Ruby's arm and peering

into Elizabeth's eyes. "I would never put my family through—I would never do such a thing." His voice cracked. "Owen changed— he made up a story. I don't know why."

Griffith shook his head. Until a few moments ago, he hadn't known a barn even existed behind the warehouse. Neither had Ruby or Graham. Upon entering, their father had told them that on some afternoons he would steal away for a few minutes and take naps in the stalls. What else didn't he know about his father? What other secrets was he keeping from them?

Peering down at the bales of hay in the empty horse stalls, Griffith covered his frown. It was too painful to look at his father for more than a few seconds; he couldn't stand seeing him so distraught. But how could he not look distraught? Within the last hour, Guy Payne had learned his brother had informed his family he'd been killed. Then he'd learned that same brother—his only brother—had passed away.

"When did he die?" Guy asked, his voice grim.

"Just the other day," Ruby answered.

"Last weekend." Elizabeth reached for her husband's hand. "It was awful, honey. There was an attack at Happy's in New Orleans." She swallowed. "Owen was terribly weak even before and . . . I don't know how much time he had left anyway, but he didn't deserve . . ." Her voice trailed off. She let go of Guy's hand and rested it on Truman's back. "This hound acted heroically, the kids tell me. But I wasn't there when . . ."

Guy trembled with the news that Griffith, Ruby, and Graham had been present at Owen's death. Just like he'd trembled for most of the trip from Camden Station.

Hiding in the back of the horse-drawn carriage, the Paynes, Josiah, and Truman traveled in silence from the downtown train depot to the storage facility behind Guy's furniture business. Several times en route Ruby had tried to ask her father questions, but he wouldn't answer, insisting that they wait until they reached their destination before speaking.

Nevertheless, Guy did reveal they were heading for the barn behind his office. The Chancellor was well aware that he'd escaped; his thugs had already searched Guy's warehouse and office twice. Guy had been on site both times, but was able to remain hidden from view, taking refuge in the trees. Guy hadn't even let the employees who were watching over his offices know he was in the vicinity, fearing it would put them at risk. After the second search, Guy didn't think the Chancellor's men would return for a third visit, but he couldn't be absolutely certain.

When they'd all arrived at the warehouse,

Guy's employees had been astonished to see him. Like the Rough Riders and the Paynes, they'd attended Guy's funeral earlier in the summer. One worker even fainted when Guy stepped through the doorway.

"You offered yourself as collateral when the Chancellor threatened Uncle Owen?" Ruby asked, struggling to understand.

Guy's eyes widened. "You know about the Chancellor threatening Uncle Owen?"

"We know about everything," Graham answered.

Out of the corner of his eye, Guy caught a glimpse of Josiah. He sat directly behind Ruby and Graham, his head lowered. The old man's gnarled hands shielded his face. But even though most of his features were hidden by his fingers, Guy found it astonishing how little the old man had changed since the day he had delivered baby Graham and the baseball safely home.

"Yes," Guy answered. "While Owen tried to come up with the money, I remained in the Chancellor's custody."

"Why would he accept you as collateral?" Ruby pressed, slipping her hand into her empty pocket.

"The Chancellor doesn't really care about money," added Griffith. "Why would he want you?"

"Mr. Griffith is correct," Josiah spoke up, the first words he'd uttered in the hayloft. "This is not about money. If it were, the Chancellor would've just as easily taken your business as security."

Guy paused. "I suppose." He faced Graham. "Since you know about everything, I'm sure you know he was interested in you."

Graham nodded once.

"Of course, neither Owen nor I would reveal your identity, but you are the reason he probably agreed to take me. He figured—"

"What did the Chancellor have to gain by accepting your offer?" Ruby interrupted. "And why did you make the offer in the first place?" The questions she hadn't been allowed to ask on the carriage ride poured out. "You were away for two months. What did you plan on telling your family when—"

"Ruby, please." Guy placed his rugged hand against her cheek and wiped her tears with a finger.

With his palm, Griffith wiped away his own tears. His sister had all the same questions that he did. None of the pieces seemed to fit. Or did they? He wanted to understand. He was beginning to wonder if he ever would.

"You're asking all the right questions." Guy kissed her forehead. "Give me the chance to answer them. I believe I can." He looked from child to child to child. "With me in his custody, the Chancellor was willing to give

Owen until the end of the year. I prayed and prayed that Owen would somehow manage to get the money, that the Chancellor would accept it, and that he'd leave us alone." Guy let out a long breath. "By offering myself, I was buying Owen time." He grit his teeth and stared at Elizabeth. "That was our plan. Owen promised to tell you all that."

"But he didn't," she said, shaking her head.

"Why?" asked Ruby.

Guy paused as Truman, who'd been lying behind Ruby and Griffith, labored to his paws, hobbled across the hay, and sat down beside him. The hound rested his head on Guy's thigh as he often did with Griffith.

"Maybe Owen thought our situation was hopeless," Guy said. He paused again. "Or maybe he thought the Chancellor was going to harm me no matter what, and he felt it would be easier . . . easier for you to believe

I'd been killed in an accident than murdered by . . ." His voice broke.

"How did the Chancellor take you?" Ruby's questions kept coming. As difficult as it was to see her father like this, she needed answers.

"We met on a boat in Chesapeake Bay, close to the harbor here in Baltimore." Guy ran his hand along his windpipe. "Owen and I were terrified to meet him in such a locale, but the Chancellor insisted." He took his wife's hand. "Owen didn't accompany me out on the boat, Liz. They made him stay behind. I bid my brother farewell on the pier." He squeezed her hand. "He was supposed to assure you I'd be okay." Guy swallowed. "I'm so sorry."

"Those were Uncle Owen's last words to us," Ruby said, glancing at Griffith. "He apologized."

"He told us to tell you he was sorry," Griffith added.

"He spoke in the present tense," said Ruby, nodding. "Now we see why. He knew there was a chance you were still alive." She lifted the necklace out from under her collar. "He gave me his keys."

"When he was dying?" Guy furrowed his brow and leaned in.

"Just before," Ruby answered. "He touched them. He was trying to tell me something. He was—"

"Dad, what did the Chancellor do to you?" Griffith interrupted. He nervously wrapped his fingers around strands of hay.

Guy sat back up and placed a hand against his head. "Griff, I was a POW, a prisoner of war. That's what it felt like. I'll spare you all the details—"

"No," Elizabeth cut him off, her voice stern. "Guy, we don't keep secrets anymore."

"After all we've been through," Graham put in, "we can handle it."

Guy managed a smile. He reached over and ruffled Graham's hair. "I'm just being a protective father."

"What did the Chancellor do to you?" Ruby repeated Griffith's question.

"At first I was shackled to a wall, but after a couple days, they unchained me."

"Where did they keep you?" Ruby and Graham asked at the same time.

"In a tiny, dark cell. No larger than a closet." Guy squeezed the back of his neck. "I have no idea how long I was in there. Ten days? Twenty? I lost track." Guy let out another long breath. "They tried to get information from me. Many times. About Graham, about the baseball, anything. But I told them nothing."

"You were alone?" asked Graham.

Guy nodded. "I barely said a single word, but I did listen to the Chancellor's men. They weren't exactly discreet. Sometimes they'd

"I was shackled to a wall."

speak right outside my cell like I wasn't even there." He looked at Josiah. "It was then that I learned this was all about control, control of the great game of baseball."

"I know that better than anyone, Mr. Guy," Josiah said, pinching his wire-framed glasses. "That is what my son covets."

Guy flinched. "Your son?" Then he began to smile. It was as if all of a sudden the pieces of a complex puzzle had snapped into place for him.

"That explains so much," he said, nodding. "I always suspected a connection. Now I know."

"Mr. Guy, he believes it's his destiny to rule the game." Josiah rested a hand on Graham's back. "He wants this prodigy."

"He has the baseball, Dad," Graham whispered.

"What?" Guy braced himself on the wooden beam by his side. The color drained from his face. "How did he get it?"

"During the attack," answered Griffith. "One of his men grabbed it."

Guy opened his mouth to speak, but when the words didn't come, he buried his face in his hands.

Griffith placed his hand on his father's back. He could feel him shaking.

"Don't worry," Ruby said, tugging on her father's pant leg. "We'll get our baseball back."

"I believe them, Mr. Guy," Josiah said, his eyes twinkling. "I've learned not to under-estimate your children."

Guy lowered his hands, rested them on Truman's torso, and managed a smile. He mouthed a thank-you.

"Mr. Guy," Josiah went on, "it is critical that we get that baseball. I cannot stress that enough." He let out a gentle cough. "I've always feared what could happen if he ever managed to get his hands on it."

"Since he has the ball, do you think he's capable of *things*?" Griffith asked, recalling the discussion he'd had with his brother and sister on the train to Atlanta.

"It's very possible, Mr. Griffith," Josiah replied anxiously. "Though I'm most concerned about Mr. Graham." He gazed at the youngest Payne. "No matter what, we mustn't let him get to you."

"He won't," Griffith stated flatly.

Josiah turned back to Guy. "Like I've told the others, I raised my son to believe he was the prodigy. But alas, it was your son who was in fact the chosen one." He spoke somberly. "My child sees himself as a failure, one who could not live up to his baseball destiny. But now he believes he has found a way to do it." He paused. "He feels he has suffered a grave injustice, and I am partly to blame. Yes, I made him feel unloved."

"He'll never feel worthiness without first

feeling love," Guy said. "Riches and power won't bring him that."

"That is correct, Mr. Guy." Josiah nodded. "You know that, I know that, and your loving family knows that. Unfortunately, my son does not." He cleared his throat and patted his chest. "He has set his sights on what he feels is the original source of his troubles: baseball. I believe he is of the mind that if he can exert control over the game, perhaps by assembling the greatest team ever known, he will no longer be a failure. Somehow he thinks that will make him the man he was supposed to be, even without setting foot on the field."

Griffith shook his head. "There's something else you're not telling us."

Josiah smiled. "You are quite perceptive, Mr. Griffith." He traced his fingers along the creases that lined his forehead. "He seeks revenge. On me, of course, and on young

Mr. Graham, the person to whom I bestowed the baseball."

Lifting Truman's snoot from his leg, Guy stood up and shuffled across the hayloft. When he reached the porthole window beyond the ladder, he stared out for a long moment. Then he turned back around, grabbing the rafter above his head with both weathered hands.

"No matter how monstrously the Chancellor behaves," Guy said, "he still has a conscience. I believe that."

"I don't," Elizabeth snapped. "Not for one second." She grabbed a handful of hay and flung it over the edge. "I've seen what he's tried to do this family, *our* family. That man has no conscience."

While he didn't agree with his wife, Guy knew better than to argue. So instead, he continued with his tale.

"I needed to escape," he said, "but I knew

if I failed, the punishment would be cruel and lethal. I would have one chance and one chance only. So I needed to be patient."

"How did you do it?" Ruby leaned forward.

"I learned their routines. I was fed twice daily, once in the morning, once in the evening. A single guard delivered my rations. In the mornings the meal came before dawn, and I always pretended to be sleeping. But I was really watching, learning. I was able to become familiar with the grounds, too. Each time they escorted me from my cell to the toilet, and whenever they brought me to the offices for questioning, I took careful notes in my head."

"You plotted your escape step-by-step," Griffith said.

"I did." Guy sat back down alongside his wife. "As the days passed, the Chancellor's guards became less diligent, even careless.

I had many opportunities to flee, but I still waited. I couldn't launch my escape plan until I was ready for every possible scenario."

"How did you know when it was time?" asked Ruby.

"Some things you just know," Griffith whispered, but not loud enough for anyone to hear.

"One morning I overpowered the guard," Guy went on. "Leaped off my cot and hit him something awful with the serving tray. I taped his mouth closed with a belt and sock, took his suit, stole his keys, and locked him in my cell."

"You wore one of the dark suits!" Graham exclaimed. "That's genius, Dad."

Guy ruffled Graham's hair again. "The escape was surprisingly easy. No one stopped me or said a word. No one knew it was me in that dark suit, not even some of the guards who'd been watching my cell. Of course, my heart was beating as fast as it had been on San Juan Hill, but everything went better than planned."

"Hadn't the Chancellor taken you somewhere by boat?" Griffith asked.

"He had," Guy replied. "That's when things turned harrowing. I had to swim across the harbor, Griff. I'd never had to swim so far in my entire life, and I didn't know if I could make it. But you know what kept me going? The thought of all of you." His voice cracked. "The thought of you enabled me to persevere. You kept me alive."

Elizabeth squeezed her husband's hand. "You don't have to continue if you don't want to." She kissed him gently on the cheek and wiped the corners of his eyes with her thumb. "If this is too much, you can tell us the rest later."

"No, Liz," said Guy, shaking his head. "I want you to hear everything now. Once they learned I'd escaped, I was in the race of my life to find you before he did. I was—I was hysterical."

"Were you looking for us in Baltimore the whole time?" Graham asked. "We didn't get here until today."

"I escaped more than two weeks ago, Grams." Guy shook his head. "Thanks to the loose lips of the Chancellor's guards, I knew the Travelin' Nine's schedule. So I headed straight for Minnesota."

"You were in Minneapolis!" Graham exclaimed, pointing at Griffith and Ruby. "I knew it!"

"I traveled only at night. It was safer that way, especially when I was on foot and not riding the rails. I didn't know if I was being followed, but I always had to assume that I was. I slept during the days, though never restfully. I wouldn't allow myself to fall into a deep slumber. Drifting in and out of consciousness, I would have these bizarre dreams."

Graham opened his mouth to speak, but Guy continued before he could utter a syllable.

"One time I had this vision where I was floating on the Mississippi, and I saw you." He looked at Graham. "But I couldn't have been, because in the hallucination time had stopped. That's what happened on San Juan Hill in Cuba, and the next thing I knew I was—"

"I had the same dream," Graham interrupted.

"The same?"

"Well, not exactly the same, but one just like it." Graham glanced at Griffith. "It had to have happened around the same time as yours."

"It's possible." Guy stroked Truman's head. The hound had once again cozied up against his leg. "That vision or dream or whatever it was has haunted me ever since. It took me back to Cuba and—"

"We know all about Cuba," Graham broke in again.

"Woody told me," added Griffith. "Dad, Grammy told us about his dream. It sounds like the one you're telling us about, but we didn't completely believe him."

"I believed it," Graham said with certainty. "Time stopped, Dad, and I saw you. It had to be you, but—but at the same time, it couldn't be—because it was impossible."

"And scary," Ruby stated. "We couldn't figure out what was real and what wasn't."

"It was scary for me, too." Guy rubbed his eyes. "Which is why I was so devastated that I didn't make it to Minneapolis in time. I wanted to be there for Graham's birthday."

Graham folded his arms tightly across his chest and looked at his brother and sister. Somehow the line between dream and reality had been crossed. He couldn't explain it, and neither could his father, but something inexplicable had occurred in Minneapolis. Just like something beyond comprehension had happened to Guy in Cuba.

Lowering his eyes, Graham stared at his sister's empty pocket. There was no denying the power of the baseball. All the hunches and beliefs he'd had—even the ones he'd been told *not* to believe—had been right. There would be no more doubting his instincts.

Ever.

"I was too late in St. Louis, too," Guy continued, "and I couldn't just keep missing you. So I decided to head back to Washington to find Owen. Of course, he was gone."

"Before Crazy Feet left the team, he said something to Uncle Owen," Ruby said. "Maybe it had to—"

"Crazy Feet left the team?" Guy's face went blank. "Did something happen to him?"

The Paynes fell silent.

"He had to leave the team," Elizabeth said, frowning. "He was spying on us for the Chancellor."

"The Chancellor forced him to choose between his family and us," Griffith added.

Guy grimaced. "That sounds exactly like something the Chancellor would do."

"Crazy Feet put us in danger," Elizabeth explained. "He admitted that what he did was wrong. He went to try to find his family."

"Before Crazy Feet left the team, he said something to Uncle Owen," Ruby repeated. "He whispered something in his ear, but we never found out what."

"Maybe he learned that you escaped," Griffith said. He let out a long breath. "Dad, the Chancellor said something to me, also."

"You've spoken with the Chancellor?" Guy's face went pale again.

"In Chicago." Griffith glanced at his sister and then back at his father. "He threatened me."

"He said to Griff, 'I have *more* than one thing you want,'" Ruby put in. "Did he mean you and Uncle Owen? But he wasn't holding Uncle Owen—"

"Or Mr. Crazy Feet?" Josiah asked. "I believe that other thing might well have been Mr. Crazy Feet."

"Or he could've been lying." Ruby flipped the hair off her neck. "I always thought he was bluffing, just trying to scare us."

"When I was his prisoner," said Guy, "he told many falsehoods. The Chancellor has no qualms about playing with the truth. He misled me on several occasions."

Josiah traced his fingers along the creases of his forearm. "My son has become the type of man who would do anything to achieve an objective. He's prone to rash and harsh acts."

"I wouldn't put anything past him." Guy nodded. "I'm afraid he may even try something at Owen's funeral."

As soon as he uttered the word "funeral," Griffith, Ruby, and Graham lowered their heads. The reunion with their father had distracted them from thinking about it for a short time.

"A military funeral will be too dangerous," Guy went on. "It would call too much attention." He swallowed. "And he can't be buried next to me, wherever you buried me. They'd expect that, too."

"Doc Lindy is taking care of the funeral arrangements," said Elizabeth. "Knowing Doc, everything's in order."

"Without a doubt," Guy agreed.

"We still need to find out about these." Ruby twirled the keys dangling around her neck.

"They might hold the *key* to something,"

Graham said, chuckling. "Get it? The *key* to something."

"Good one, Grams." Ruby playfully shoved her brother and rolled her eyes. "How long did it take you to come up with that?"

"You should see these three," Elizabeth said, drawing a circle in the air around her children. "They kid and tease each other mercilessly, but they look out for one another with ferocity. You'd be so proud."

"I'm already proud," said Guy.

"We need to find out what's in Uncle Owen's storage trunk." Ruby couldn't keep the impatience from her voice.

"We do," Guy agreed, "but we shouldn't all go together."

"We're not splitting up," Elizabeth said, shaking her head. "I don't want this family separated again."

Guy reached for his wife's hand. "It will only be for a short while, Liz," he assured her. "You know we shouldn't all go."

"I just hate the thought of not—"

"Me too." Guy wove his fingers into hers. "We'll be together again soon." He looked at Josiah. "I will go to my brother's with Ruby. You and Elizabeth will stay here with the boys."

"We shouldn't stay in the barn, Mr. Guy," Josiah said. "Not without you here. I do not feel that would be wise."

Guy nodded. "On the way to Uncle Owen's, we'll stop by the house. We'll leave you with the Rough Riders. That will be safer." He paused. "But we'll wait till morning. We've traveled enough for one day."

"I like that plan better," said Elizabeth. "But I still hate the thought of splitting up."

Guy squeezed his wife's hand. "Liz, we'll only be apart for a few hours. I'll never leave you again. I promise."

8

★

The Keys to the Trunk

arly the next morning Guy and Ruby left the others with the Rough Riders and headed off to Uncle Owen's. Upon arriving at the house, they were greeted by a most unwelcome sight.

"I don't like the way this looks," Guy said, walking up the narrow path to the front door, a door suspiciously ajar. "Stay close." He extended his arm so that Ruby would remain a few steps behind, and, with his boot, gently kicked it open.

Ruby gasped. "What happened?"

"Oh, no," Guy whispered.

"It looks like a stampede of animals charged through," she said.

Guy took Ruby's hand as they headed into the foyer.

The living room had been ransacked. The legs of the large wooden coffee table by the sofa had been snapped, and all the sofa's cushions had been cut open, leaving a coating of fabric and stuffing everywhere. The stack of logs next to the fireplace had been toppled, and it appeared that one of the logs had been thrown through the octagonal stained-glass window in the corner. The mirror that hung over the hearth had been shattered, its remains scattered on the sliced-up leather chair in the corner.

"What do you think they were looking for?" Ruby whispered.

Her father didn't respond.

"Do you think they're still here?"

Guy shook his head and pointed to the puddles on the windowsill and along the base-boards. "Those are from rain, but we haven't had any since earlier in the week. This happened days ago."

The destruction in the kitchen was just as bad. All the cabinets had been opened, glasses and plates smashed. All four chairs were knocked over, legs broken. Two of the window-panes that looked out into the backyard were missing, and because of the rain, water had pooled on the counter. Several crates of papers had been dumped on the floor.

"These are old financial records," Guy said, examining the papers.

Turning toward the back door, Ruby let out a deep sigh. The door was still locked. Whoever had been here—not that she had any doubt who it was—hadn't searched outside.

Ruby let go of her father's hand, stepped over the rubble, and opened the door. As she headed outside, she lifted the chain of keys from under her collar. When she reached the picnic table, she stopped.

"This is where we sat with Uncle Owen the night of the funeral," Ruby said. Guy had followed her outside. "We were right here when he gave us the baseball." She ran her fingers along the bench and stared up at her father. "Mom was so mad at Uncle Owen that night. I'd never seen her so upset."

Guy cringed. "I'm so sorry I put you through that."

"We know you are," Ruby whispered. She led him to the corner of the yard.

The trunk was hidden from sight. The brush around it had grown considerably, and unless someone knew to look for the storage bin, they'd never have found it.

Ruby lifted the keys from around her neck and passed them to her father.

"You nervous?" he asked, pushing aside the branches and weeds.

"A little," Ruby replied.

Tilting up the lock, Guy inserted a key. It didn't turn. He tried a second one. It did. He motioned with his head for Ruby to step closer. Then he raised the heavy lid, banging one of the side hinges with his fist so that it would open all the way.

"It's empty," Guy said.

"No, it's not." Ruby pointed.

Taped to the underside of the cover, in the corner along the edge, was an envelope. Instantly Ruby knew why it was there. If the

trunk had been discovered, the envelope could have gone unnoticed, especially if it was dark.

She pulled off the envelope. "'For My Brother,'" she said, reading the words on the outside. The handwriting was Uncle Owen's.

"Open it," said Guy.

"It's addressed to you." She held it out to her father.

"He wanted you to find it. He gave you the keys."

"He only gave me the keys because . . ." Ruby stopped.

Guy sighed. He took the envelope. "We'll read it together." He unfolded the paper and draped his arm around his daughter.

Guy,
    I don't know how to begin this letter other than with these three words:

    I am sorry.

Sluggers

I am writing this in case something happens to me, and I fear that something will. Something terrible is on my horizon, and thus I need to tell you things, in case I never get the chance to in person. If what I fear does indeed occur, please make sure I am laid to rest in our place so that you will always remember our Sundays with the family.

Family.

I misled your family, Guy. After leaving you on the bay, I had second thoughts. I wondered—doubted—if the Rough Riders, such men of honor, would go along with the plan. Would they help if they knew you were alive? I feared they'd consider this a family problem. Or worse, my problem, one I should deal with on my own. However, I thought that if the Rough Riders saw Elizabeth as a widow and her children as fatherless, they'd be spurred to act. Not only would they help, they'd do everything in their power. Hence, after bidding you farewell and then seeing Elizabeth all alone, a force inside me took hold. So I lied.

I lied.

I regretted it the moment I did, but those were words I could not take back. Never did I envision things would spiral out of control so quickly. I should've realized the implications of my untruth. I should've. I should have realized how many lives you've touched. But I didn't. All I could do was hope that one day the loan would be paid back and that you'd return. Yes, you'd be furious and disappointed and sad and hurt, but you are my brother. You would forgive me. Again. You always did, Guy.

Please forgive me.

I have faults. I am impulsive. I act in haste. I gamble. I have loose lips. However, I am an honorable person. And I try. Best that I can.

It was not easy returning to life as damaged goods. But I never gave up. Appreciate and understand the agony of this veteran.

Guy, I did what I thought was best for the family, but I did more harm than good. I thought I could somehow make up for my earlier bad deeds.

I was wrong. I am sorry.

Love, Owen

9

★

Baltimore Boys

alfway down the block, Griffith watched his younger brother hand out fliers to the passersby. Scribe stood alongside him, and his tremendous size was clearly intimidating some of the pedestrians, but the mountain of a man was not about to leave Graham's side.

Before heading off to promote Wednesday's match, the barnstormers had devised several extra safety precautions. The two Payne boys were each assigned shadows. Scribe and Bubbles accompanied Graham along the streets by the harbor, while Doc stayed with Griffith on the pier. Happy, unable to stand for long stretches, provided an additional lookout by watching the crowds from a bench at the edge of the dock. Elizabeth kept an eye out from a bench three over from the old-timer. And before the group had even headed into town, they'd decided that Josiah would remain at the Paynes' house; they feared his distinctive look would cause him to stand out too much.

"Here you go, gentlemen," Griffith said, holding out fliers to a group of approaching businessmen.

"No, thank you," said one man. He tapped the sheet in Griffith's hand as he passed. "Already plan on being there."

"Me too," said a second man, declining the flier with a wave.

"My kids are making me take the afternoon off," a third businessman said. He took a paper. "Game's at two, right?" he asked.

"Yes, sir," Griffith replied. He then turned to Doc. "Looks like you did a great job of promoting the game even before we got to town."

"I can't exactly take the credit," Doc said. He scratched the stubble on his chin with a flier. "The Baltimore ballists are the ones who got the word out. Them boys did a week's worth of advertising in a single day! I was too busy making funeral arrangements. They helped with that, too."

Upon arriving in Baltimore, Doc had contacted the Baltimore Bombers and informed them of the changed circumstances. Responding like gentlemen, the local ballists offered their assistance. First they provided names of people who could help coordinate Uncle Owen's funeral. Then they took care of reserving a field for the match; since the hometown Orioles, Baltimore's professional team, had an off day, the local players were able to secure Union Park. Finally they created the fliers and started spreading the news.

"I got some more fliers here," Woody said.

Griffith and Doc turned to see Woody, swinging the satchel as he joined them at the end of the pier. Elizabeth and Happy followed several steps behind.

"We can watch the crowd much better from out here," said Happy. "And I'm tired of sitting. I may not be able to do some of the things I used to, but I'm still perfectly capable of standing on my own two feet for a little while."

"Many people have already heard about the game," Griffith said to his mother. He glanced across the street to Graham, still easy to spot with Scribe next to him. "We're going to have a huge crowd on Wednesday."

"It's wonderful," Elizabeth said, waving

the fliers at the blue sky. "The funeral is going to take up most of tomorrow, so this will be our only chance to let folks know about the match."

Griffith approached a woman who appeared to be a teacher, walking with a group of young students.

"Here's some fliers for your class," he said.

"Thank you, young man," said the teacher.

"There's a coupon on each one," Griffith explained, pointing to the paper. "Present the flier when you buy your ticket, and you get a free souvenir flag."

"Wonderful," she replied. "Perhaps my principal will allow us to leave school early and head over together."

"Nothing beats a field trip to the ballpark," said Griffith, grinning. "Baseball is a great learning experience!"

• • •

With Scribe and Bubbles a couple of strides behind, Graham headed toward the group of boys playing baseball down the side street. Unlike the crowded thoroughfare in front of the harbor, the boys were the only ones on this block, and since there weren't any wagons or horses, either, they were able to play in the middle of the road.

As he walked along the edge of the curb, Graham gazed up at the apartments lining both sides of the street. The redbrick buildings seemed to trap the heat; it was much hotter here than on the pier. Clotheslines filled with laundry hung from windows, stretching from one side of the street to the other. Pulling his collar over his face, Graham breathed through his mouth. Over by the water, the smell of rotting fish had made him queasy, but here the stench was even worse, thanks to the mounds of trash and manure piled next to many of the doorways. More than likely, the boys had the street to themselves because no one else could endure the odor.

Graham stepped off the sidewalk and, without breaking stride, headed onto the makeshift baseball diamond. Crossing the infield, he walked straight to the mound. As he neared, Graham saw that the boys were older; they looked to be about Griffith's age.

"We're in the middle of a game," the hurler snapped. "Do you mind?"

Graham held out the flier.

"What's this?" The hurler snatched the paper.

A few of the others gathered around to read the sheet.

"You should come," Graham said, looking around at the boys.

"We live near Union Park," one boy said, peering at the paper over the pitcher's shoulder.

"I've heard these Travelin' Nine ballists

DIAMOND: *infield.*

119

"I'm ready!"

are supposed to be pretty good," said another.

"Pretty good?" Graham scrunched his face into a knot. "Trust me, you'll never see a team play—"

"I'm ready! Pitch the ball!"

Everyone turned.

At the line, a button-nosed boy, grinning from ear to ear, wagged his timber.

"I was just telling them about a match on Wednesday," Graham called to the boy.

"Wednesday? I'm playing in a match right now!" The beaming boy fidgeted, unable to control his excitement. "It's finally my turn to strike. These guys always make me hit last because I'm the youngest. I'm only four and a half."

Graham took a few strides toward the dish. The boy at the line was bigger than any four-and-a-half-year-old he'd ever seen, but closer up, Graham could see he was actually much younger than his size suggested.

THE LINE:
the batter's box.

TIMBER:
baseball bat.

STRIKE (v.):
to swing.

DISH:
home plate.

121

"You should come watch the game too," Graham urged.

"Watch?" said the boy, still flashing his supersize smile. "Who wants to watch baseball? I want to *play* baseball."

"He's going to be real good someday," the hurler said, turning back to Graham. "Sometimes when he connects, he hits the pill farther than any of us, and we're more than twice his age. My pop thinks if he ever takes the game seriously, he could be real special." The hurler flipped the ball into the air. "But when I'm on the hill, most of the time he ends up missing by a mile and corkscrewing himself into the ground!"

Graham looked back at the boy. Watching him take his practice cuts, Graham was reminded of himself. The feisty kid couldn't contain his enthusiasm.

"Bring him with you to the game," Graham told the hurler. "He'll enjoy it more than he thinks."

PILL: baseball. Also called "rock" (see page 170) or "rawhide" (see page 170).

HILL: pitcher's mound. Also called "bump" (see page 190).

CUTS: swings.

The hurler nodded. "He comes with us wherever we go. At first we didn't like it, but the kid grows on you. There's something about him."

"Step aside," the boy called. He wagged his bat at Graham and then smiled mischievously. "Watch me hit one to the harbor."

The hurler covered his mouth with his mitt so the boy couldn't hear what he was saying to Graham. "He probably could," he said, "but don't tell him that. We'll never hear the end of it." Then he added, "You want to bat next?"

Graham peered over at Scribe and Bubbles, standing against the brick building in front of first bag. Bubbles was pointing to his timepiece and motioning across the pier.

"I wish I could," Graham replied, "but I have to meet my family. I can't even stick around to see him hit. Hopefully, I'll get to one day."

MITT:
baseball glove.
Also called
"leather" (see
page 151).

BAG:
base. Also called
"sack" (see page
151).

123

A STAR-SPANGLED CELEBRATION!

The 75th Anniversary of Our National Anthem!

AMERICA'S SONG! AMERICA'S PASTIME!

American Heroes!

the Travelin' Nine

— versus —

the Baltimore Bombers

Date: WEDNESDAY, SEPTEMBER 13

Location: UNION PARK **Game Time:** TWO O'CLOCK

Admission: 50 CENTS

✪ ✪ ✪ BONUS COUPON ✪ ✪ ✪

Bring this coupon to the match and receive

a souvenir American flag upon entrance into the stadium!

They were fulfilling Uncle Owen's final request.

10

★

Funeral for a Fallen Hero

wen Payne has made his final trip around the bases," Preacher Wil said, standing in front of the coffin. "He's rounded third and headed for home one last time."

Flipping the hair off her neck and fanning her face with a leftover flier from the day before, Ruby looked at the ballists gathered in a semicircle around Preacher Wil. The Travelin' Nine all wore their Sunday best, and in a showing of team unity, they had on their team caps as well. Ruby and her brothers were dressed up too. The three had on the same outfits they'd worn to the other funeral earlier in the summer. It was the first time they'd worn these clothes since that awful day, an afternoon in which the heat and humidity had been just as unbearable.

Ruby exhaled a long breath. They may have been uncomfortably hot, but at least they were safe. They didn't have to worry about being discovered by the Chancellor's men in this remote locale. No one would ever figure a war hero would be laid to rest in such a secluded cemetery.

"Of all of us gathered here today," Preacher Wil continued, "I knew Owen Payne for the shortest time. Even less than you." He nodded to Josiah. "But sometimes such a *tabula rasa*, such a clean slate, allows one greater clarity, or as I've heard uttered these last weeks, allows one to see the things that others don't." He held his prayer book to his chest. "In Owen Payne I saw a man of great faith who loved his family." He lifted an arm to the heavens. "I saw a man of courage and conviction. I saw a man who sought forgiveness."

Forgiveness.

Preacher Wil's last words echoed in Ruby's head. They were meant for Uncle Owen, but they could just as easily be applied to Crazy Feet. Had the others recognized it too? And when Preacher Wil glanced at Josiah, she wondered if he was *telling* him that his words were intended for him as well.

Did they also apply to the Chancellor?

Raising her forearm, Ruby shielded her eyes from the sun, rising above the trees beyond the river and reflecting off the coffin's brass molding. The early morning rays cast long shadows from the headstones and figurines throughout the hillside cemetery. She gazed at the meadow below. They were fulfilling Uncle Owen's final request, burying him in his favorite place in the world. In her mind's eye, she pictured her uncle and father as boys, playing catch almost in this very spot. A hint of a smile crept onto Ruby's face. Around the bend was where she and her brothers went fishing with their father on Sunday afternoons. That was her favorite place.

"Let's swing hard in case we hit it!" Guy Payne declared.

Ruby spun around. Preacher Wil was no longer standing before the group. Her father was. So deep in her daydream, Ruby hadn't heard the conclusion of Preacher Wil's eulogy. She hoped she hadn't missed any of her father's.

"When we were boys," Guy said in a booming voice, "our father always told us to swing hard, and Owen sure did. In every endeavor, every life experience, my brother gave it his all." Guy cleared his throat and peered around at his fellow veterans. Then his eyes settled on his children. "The brave know only of forgiveness. That's something else our father told us, and as I look at the group assembled here, I know of no others on this great earth who are any braver. So I ask that you look into your souls and apply those words to my brother." He gazed around at the Rough Riders again, this time allowing his eyes to rest on each soldier for a moment. "But don't stop there. I challenge you to go further. Think about Crazy Feet. Think about the opponents you have faced on the ball field and the enemies you have encountered on the battlefield." He faced Elizabeth. "And think about the one who wishes to bring such harm. Yes, think even of him in terms of forgiveness, for the brave know only of forgiveness."

The hint of a smile returned to Ruby's

face. It was almost as if her father had heard her thoughts.

She looked over at Truman, sitting up tall beside Griffith. She remembered what Griffith had said about the hound, how Truman seemed to forgive both Crazy Feet and Uncle Owen before anyone else had. His love was unconditional, his affection more than a person could ever offer.

Then Ruby glanced over at her mother. Standing with her arms folded, Elizabeth stared back at her husband. Her face held a blank expression, just as it had when Guy commenced his speech. She wasn't ready to forgive Uncle Owen and Crazy Feet, and certainly not the Chancellor. She couldn't completely forgive her husband, either.

But Ruby knew she would, eventually. That was her way. Just as people grieve at different speeds, people forgive at different speeds.

"As all of you know," Guy went on, "this is where Owen and I used to play ball." He pointed to the meadow and waited for the ballists to face the grassy clearing. "This was our field of dreams. Owen and I dreamed here, dreamed big. We promised each other we'd travel the world over, discover new lands, and make our family proud. Right here is where Owen and I vowed we'd meet *all* of life's challenges."

Guy placed his cap over his heart and took a few steps toward the meadow. The Travelin' Nine removed their caps too. Then the barnstormers stood in silence. After several minutes, Guy turned around and placed his hat back on his head. The sun shone over his shoulder. All anyone could see was his outline—his silhouette—as he addressed the group.

"Now we face our greatest challenge of all," Guy said. "This challenge will rival what we encountered on San Juan Hill. Because this one is personal, so deeply personal. It is a fight for our family." He looked around at each of the ballists again. "But in many ways too we are fighting once more for our nation. Our nation's game. Baseball is meant to be a part of this great land for generations. That's something I believe with all my heart. This game of baseball represents the resilience of America. We do not back down from a fight or yield to challenges." Guy walked over to his brother's coffin and kissed the lid. "We will stand tall. We will prevail. Huzzah."

"Huzzah!"

11

★

Game Day!

hat a day for baseball!" Happy exclaimed as the barnstormers walked along 25th Street toward Union Park.

Golden sunshine filled the streets of Baltimore. A few fair-weather clouds hovered high above the rooftops, but none strayed into the sun's path. A light, steady breeze cooled the air, the gentle wind whisking away yesterday's heat and humidity.

"What a fine-looking stadium!" Doc

declared when the team turned the corner
onto Barclay Street.

Union Park had come into full view. The
stadium was decked out in patriotic glory.
Red, white, and blue bunting hung along
the brick face, which stretched an entire city
block. By the entrance, a silo-sized American
flag was suspended from tall wooden posts.
At the top of the ballpark, Old Glory and the
Maryland state flag hung from metal poles.

In an instant, the sight of the black, gold,
red, and white of Maryland's flag brought
Griffith back to Uncle Owen's funeral. The
state flag, along with an American flag, had
been draped over the coffin before it was
lowered into the earth.

But Griffith refused to allow himself to
think about the somber ceremony. Instead
he recalled the remainder of yesterday.

After Uncle Owen's funeral, everyone had
returned to the Paynes' house for a meal to

celebrate the life of Owen Payne. Bubbles spun a tale about Owen from San Antonio that involved a horse, a swarm of bees, and a pond, though most in the group wondered if it had ever happened at all. Woody said when he'd spent the trip to Cuba over the side of the boat, seasick, Owen had stayed with him the whole way.

"He literally gave me the shirt off his back," Woody proclaimed.

Then Guy shared stories about growing up with Owen. Owen had been quite the prankster. At school he'd dip the hair of ponytailed girls into inkwells. When the teacher wrote on the board, he'd sneak bites of the apple sitting on the corner of her desk. And Owen was almost always responsible whenever recess had to be extended because the teachers and students were mysteriously locked out of the school.

The meal had been joyous and festive,

exactly the way Owen would've wanted it.

"This is where the Orioles play," Griffith said to the Professor when they neared the entrance. "They won ninety-eight games last year."

"But they only came in second place," Ruby added. "Those Boston Beaneaters won a hundred and two!"

Both Griffith and Ruby told the ballists all about *their* Baltimore Orioles. Even though they'd lost the pennant the last two seasons to Boston, the Orioles were usually the best team in the league, having won the championship the three previous years. Griffith and Ruby knew the names of all the players, and Guy always took the family to at least three or four games each season. Last year they went to a game against Boston just before he'd headed off to San Antonio.

"I can't wait to see the Rough Riders take the pitch in Union Park," Graham said.

It's going to be strange not rooting for the Orioles," added Griffith.

"Just make sure you cheer for us!" Elizabeth said, smiling.

The Travelin' Nine were as excited as the kids. Tales and Doc put on their gloves several blocks before the entrance, Guy held a baseball in each hand, and every so often, Woody would jump into the air and click his boots. Even though it was still hours before game time (which explained why so few people were milling about the stadium), the barnstormers already had their first-pitch energy.

"We're finally taking the field with Guy Payne!" the Professor cried.

"We hope you can keep up with us!" Bubbles added.

The Rough Riders laughed.

"I hope so too," said Guy, grinning. "I haven't played in a while, so I may be—"

"Are you making up excuses already, honey?" Elizabeth teased. "I'm sure Graham wouldn't mind taking the field in your place if you don't think you're up for it."

"Just say the word, Dad," Graham said, leaping next to his father. "I'll gladly—"

Truman began to growl. The ballists stopped dead in their tracks.

From all directions the Chancellor's men emerged. Some approached from the stadium's entrance, a few came from behind, and others walked up from the sides, seemingly out of nowhere.

Instinctively Guy and Elizabeth jumped in front of their children. Scribe grabbed Graham's hand, while the Rough Riders formed a circle around the Payne family.

"Where did they all come from?" Ruby whispered as the dark-suited men with pink pocket squares formed a line on the sidewalk several arms' lengths away.

Suddenly the row of thugs parted, and the Chancellor stepped forward. His steely eyes locked on Josiah's.

"Old man," the Chancellor said, "your clock has stopped."

Truman's steady growl continued.

"My son," Josiah said in a gentle, barely audible voice, "it's good to stand close to you again. Believe it or not—"

"Spare me your foolish words," the Chancellor cut him off. "I gave up listening to your nonsense years ago."

"In your heart, I know you don't believe that." Josiah stood tall—as tall as he could—in the bluster of such cold words. "My son, I know goodness remains in—"

"I said, spare me your foolishness!" the Chancellor barked.

Griffith flinched. He looked around at the adults. Without question, they all wanted to leap to Josiah's defense, but to a man (and woman) they recognized it wasn't their place. How long would they be able to stand idly by though?

"You're too late, old man," the Chancellor went on, the chill in his voice growing icier. "You should never have left the mountains. You're powerless here. You were too late—"

"I do not believe that." This time Josiah interrupted his son. "I'll never believe you feel that way."

"So foolish, old man," said the Chancellor. "And don't you *ever* cut me off again." He practically spat the words.

Griffith glanced at Josiah. In spite of the old man's efforts to reach out to his son, Griffith sensed his rage. Josiah's tightly clenched fists held frustration; his reddening cheeks bespoke flaring emotions.

"I do not believe," he said, "that a man who grew up in *our* home thinks that any of this—money, power, possessions—matters."

"Delusional, too." The Chancellor laughed.

"I rejected you and your hermit lifestyle years ago." He stepped forward. "And I reject your unworldly ways again, now and forever."

"We reject you and your cowardice," Woody growled, the first Rough Rider to speak. "You killed one of ours." He beat his bowlegs.

"You attacked these children," snapped the Professor.

The Chancellor looked to the men on his right. As if the glance was a cue, both drew back their jackets, revealing weapons.

"Merely a cost of doing business," the Chancellor said matter-of-factly.

Suddenly Griffith took a step forward. "Where are the three goons who shot at us?" he asked, surprised by the power of his voice.

"They didn't follow orders, Griffith Payne," the Chancellor replied, growling the name. "They have been dealt with. Just like I'll be dealing with all of you."

Guy reached for his son, pulled him back, and stepped in front. For the first time in weeks, Guy Payne stood face-to-face with the Chancellor.

"You were a cost of doing business too," the Chancellor said, wagging a finger. "A minor expense. And your escape was of no consequence, for one of yours was mine." He waved the finger at the other Rough Riders. "He lowered your worth." The Chancellor snickered. "To nothing."

Griffith peered around at the soldiers. Doc had a hand over his mouth, Woody gnawed on a knuckle, and Bubbles was biting his tongue (literally). Once again, they all wanted to leap to the aid of one of their own, but this time it was Guy Payne's moment.

"You will not prevail," Guy said firmly.

"Your brother's debt is now officially yours, Guy Payne," the Chancellor declared, the smirk never leaving his face. "And like I told your boy, I always get my way." He faced Josiah again. "But *you* still haven't learned that. You think you matter. That's why you're here. How pathetic. My time is now. That is the lesson you will be taught."

Griffith ran a hand through his hair. Despite the threat, Griffith thought he heard something else in the Chancellor's voice: regret. Or maybe that was just something he *hoped* he'd heard. He studied Josiah. If the Chancellor's tone did contain a tinge of remorse, Josiah didn't acknowledge it. He remained rigid, as he'd been for most of the encounter.

"I am halfway there," the Chancellor said, turning back toward the Paynes, still surrounded by Rough Riders. He reached into his pocket and removed the baseball, then lowered his eyes to Graham. "And I *always* get what I want."

Feeling his brother bristle, Griffith grabbed Graham's clenched fist. At the same time, Guy placed a steady hand on Griffith's shoulder and wrapped his other arm around Ruby. The three Payne children wanted to leap at the Chancellor and rip the baseball from his grasp, but they couldn't. Not with the Chancellor's men holding guns.

"At long last," the Chancellor said, pivoting toward Josiah again, "I have this." He hovered over his father and squeezed the baseball in front of his face. "Today you will see my destiny with your own discolored eyes."

"I *always* get what I want."

12

★

A Team of All-Stars and Talkin' Baseball

ot only did the Chancellor have the baseball, but he'd also assembled a team composed of the best ballists in Baltimore.

"Half of the Orioles are playing for the Bombers," Graham growled, folding his arms tightly across his chest and glaring at the field.

"Half?" Griffith grumbled as he sized up the home squad warming up on the pitch. "I recognize *every* face. All of these ballists are either on the Orioles or used to be."

Since the Orioles had the day off, the Chancellor had borrowed their most talented players and built a team of all-stars. These ballists played smart, strategic baseball, the brand of ball the Rough Riders liked to play. The hurlers threw strikes, changed speeds, and worked the count. The strikers laid down bunts, stole bases, and executed plays like the hit-and-run to perfection. Against this opponent, if no magic was involved, the Travelin' Nine would need every bit of skill and baseball intelligence they could muster. And if the Chancellor was able to get the ball to work for him . . .

"Wilbert Robinson is a solid backstop," Griffith said to Josiah. He pointed to the Bombers' catcher warming up a hurler by the home team dugout along the first base line. Then he motioned across the diamond.

STRIKER:
batter, or hitter.

BUNT:
soft and short hit, often to advance a runner.

HIT-AND-RUN:
a play in which a batter swings at the pitch while the base runner attempts to steal a base.

BACKSTOP:
catcher.

FIRST BASE LINE:
line extending from home plate through first and all the way to the outfield. Anything within the line is considered to be in fair territory; anything outside the line is in foul territory.

149

"Hughie Jennings is a great shortstop. I wish he hadn't left Baltimore after last season."

"From the little I've seen so far," Josiah replied, "Mr. Hughie plays a bit too dirty for my taste."

"Oh, no," Happy interjected. "He's the type of hard-nosed ballist you love to have on your team." He paused. "But you *hate* playing against him."

Josiah shook his head. "I like a player who prefers to get a hit instead of getting hit by a pitch."

"I'm with Happy," said Griffith. "I want ballists who'll do whatever it takes to get on base."

"This is great!" Graham exclaimed, joining in. "I love that the three of you are arguing."

"We're not arguing, Mr. Graham," Josiah corrected him. "We're having a discussion."

Graham laughed. "Trust me, when it

comes to talking baseball, Griffith always has to have the last word. He has to win every discussion."

Happy smiled. "He's got a point."

"I'll keep that in mind, Mr. Graham."

Griffith shook his fist at his brother and then looked out at the Bombers playing catch in the outer garden. None of the players had any idea about what was really going on. Yes, they were playing for the Chancellor, but like Cy Young back in New Orleans, they weren't acting frightened or nervous.

OUTER GARDEN: *outfield.*

LEATHER: *baseball glove. Also called "mitt" (see page 123).*

HOT CORNER: *third base.*

SACK: *base. Also called "bag" (see page 123).*

"What do you think of John McGraw?" asked Josiah.

"What a batsman!" Griffith replied.

"He can flash some leather at the hot corner, too," Josiah added.

Griffith pointed to the ballist on the edge of the outer-garden grass behind second sack. "Wee Willie Keeler used to be my favorite Oriole," he said, "but he's playing for Brooklyn this year. It sure is nice to see him back."

"Why do so many teams have players nicknamed 'Wee Willie'?" Graham asked.

Griffith chuckled. "Little brother," he replied, placing a hand on Graham's shoulder, "I guarantee you the ballist who played for the Minneapolis Millers got his nickname *because* of this Wee Willie. Two years ago Wee Willie Keeler hit in forty-four straight games. That record's going to stand up for years. I guarantee that, too. He hits 'em where they ain't. That's what he tells everyone."

"He's the smallest player out there," said Graham.

"He may not be big and tall. Heck, he may even be the same size as a batboy, but he can play the game with the biggest and best of them." Griffith leaned in close. "He also plays right garden as well as Woody," he whispered.

"I reckon you shouldn't let Woody hear you say that," Graham said, imitating Woody's accent. Then he smiled his mischievous smile. "But he doesn't play it as well as the Travelin' Nine's right scout back in New Orleans!"

Griffith laughed. "How could he?" He motioned to Wee Willie Keeler again. "He's perfected the 'Baltimore Chop.'"

"Not only has he perfected it," Ruby put in, entering the conversation. She'd been talking with a group of Rough Riders at the far end of the dugout. "He's taught the rest of his teammates how to do it too."

"Last season," said Griffith, "I saw Wee Willie Keeler wrangle a double out of one."

"Are you sure?" Ruby eyed him sideways. "That sounds like a story Bubbles would tell."

"What about Bubbles?" The Travelin' Nine's shortstop walked over.

"We're just talking about . . ." Ruby

SCOUT: *outfielder. The right fielder was called the "right scout," the center fielder was called the "center scout," and the left fielder was called the "left scout."*

BALTIMORE CHOP: *when a batter hits the ball downward onto the infield surface as hard as he can so that the ball rebounds skyward.*

paused, smiling. "We're talking about your great glove and throwing arm."

"Just making sure." He handed her the lineup card. "Post this on the dugout wall."

Griffith, Ruby, and Graham huddled around the paper with the batting order.

"It's the same order as New Orleans," Graham said, "except Dad is taking my spot."

1. Guy—catcher
2. Tales—second base
3. Woody—right field
4. Scribe—center field
5. Doc—third base
6. Professor Lance—first base
7. Bubbles—shortstop
8. Preacher Wil—pitcher
9. Elizabeth—left field

"It worked well there," said Happy, peeking over their shoulders. "Why change things?"

Griffith tapped the page. "It's the lineup we agreed to on the train."

"Pretty much," Ruby said, nodding. "Woody's back in right, and Mom's over in left."

"How'd they decide who would play from behind, Mom or Dad?" Graham asked.

"I'll answer that one," Guy replied, stepping up to his children. "Because this is my first time playing with the Rough Riders since San Antonio, everyone agreed I should play my usual position. Even your mother." He turned to Elizabeth, who had also walked over.

She smiled. "I made sure to give him a few pointers."

"But I did warn everyone that I may be a little rusty and that—"

"Your father is looking for a way to exit gracefully when the Rough Riders call on me to catch after a few innings," Elizabeth interrupted with a laugh.

The three kids laughed. So did Guy. Once again their mother had the last word, and Guy knew better than to argue with her (especially since what she'd said was probably true).

Suddenly Elizabeth stopped laughing. She pointed to the area behind the Bombers' bench, and the others quieted too. During warm-ups, the Chancellor and his thugs had taken their seats out in the open in the stands. However, the Chancellor was now standing again, and he'd taken out the baseball. Staring across at the Travelin' Nine dugout, he massaged it with both hands.

Graham scrunched his face into as tight a knot as he could. He couldn't stand the sight of the Chancellor with *his* baseball. Pounding a white-knuckled fist into his thigh, Graham wanted to burst from the front steps of the dugout, tear across the green oasis, and rip the ball out of his scaly fingers.

He looked away. He *needed* to look elsewhere. The same red, white, and blue bunting that had adorned the outside of the park lined the fences that separated the stands from the field. Out beyond center garden, just like at some of the other fields on which the Travelin' Nine had played, an American flag waved proudly from a tall pole. Underneath the Stars and Stripes were three pennants, each commemorating a Baltimore Orioles championship season from the middle of the decade.

GREEN OASIS: *playing field. Also called "pitch"* (see page 26).

ROOTERS: *fans; people who cheer at ball games. Also called "cranks"* (see page 24).

Turning toward the rooters behind the visitors' dugout, Graham spotted the group of boys he'd met while distributing the fliers. Several of them, including the one who'd been pitching, were heading down the aisle. Graham smiled. The boy who'd been batting was also one of the ones bounding down the steps. He was eating a long sandwich that appeared to contain a sausage.

"I'm glad you came," Graham said, directing his words to the youngest one.

"So are we," said the hurler. "We didn't know all these Orioles would be playing."

"Neither did we," Graham muttered.

"We brought George along," another boy said. He leaned against the fence and pointed to the not-so-little boy stuffing the remainder of the odd-shaped sandwich into his mouth.

"Your name's George?" Graham asked.

The boy waved.

"I'm Graham."

Still chewing, the boy smiled.

"You're going to enjoy watching the Travelin' Nine play." Graham faced George as he spoke. "You'll learn a lot about the game, too." His voice rose and fell like Griffith's often did when he talked baseball.

"I hope they hit some home runs," George

said, wiping his mouth with a chubby fore-arm. His happy feet danced. "Four-baggers are my favorite hits of all."

"The barnstormers have some big bop-pers in their lineup," said Graham. "I'm sure they'll hit a few."

"Time to find our seats, George," the hurler said, placing two hands on the young-ster's broad shoulders. He glanced up at Graham. "We'll be looking for you during the game."

Graham waved to his new friends and then turned to his brother and sister. Ruby and Griffith had moved to the end of the bench closer to home dish. Graham headed down the dugout because out on the field, the hometown Bombers had finished taking their warm-ups, and in a matter of moments the umpire would call Guy to the line to start the match.

"We're going to do our pregame ritual," Ruby said.

FOUR-BAGGERS: home runs. Also called "round-trippers" (see page 169).

BOPPERS: players who make the most hits in the lineup.

"Even though we don't have the baseball?" asked Graham.

"We're going to include everyone," Griffith replied. "Ruby and I think if we're all together, our unity may be as powerful as—maybe even more powerful than—the baseball."

"It's worth a shot," Graham said.

Moments later the Travelin' Nine had gathered around the three Paynes. So had Josiah and Happy, as well as Truman, who'd ducked into the center of the circle. Griffith, Ruby, and Graham placed their hands atop one another. Then, one by one, the barnstormers added their hands to the pile. Even Truman raised a paw.

"As everyone knows," Graham began as soon as all the hands (and paw) were joined together, "Griffith, Ruby, and I always held the baseball before the start of each game." He took a deep breath. "We don't have the

Even Truman raised a paw.

baseball this afternoon, but we have one another. We believe that's more powerful than any object."

"Be together," Griffith and Ruby said as one. "Always."

13

★

First-Inning Fireworks

Standing alongside the ballists in the dugout, the three Payne kids and Elizabeth watched as Guy Payne stepped to the line for his first at bat as a member of the Travelin' Nine. He tipped his cap to the umpire and backstop, nodded to the southpaw hurler, and then shifted his boots into position alongside the dish.

"He has the same batting stance as you," Elizabeth said, resting her hand on Graham's shoulder.

STEP TO THE LINE (*v.*): to prepare to hit.

SOUTHPAW: left-handed individual; the commonly used nickname for players who throw left-handed.

"Well, let's just hope he does better than I did my first time up."

Unfortunately, Guy was just as over-anxious as Graham had been. He mistimed the first pitch—an outside slider that would have been a ball—and swung early for strike one. Swinging late on the next pitch, he quickly found himself in a two-strike hole. Needing to collect himself, Guy stepped off the line and took several practice cuts before shuffling back to the dish.

SLIDER: a pitch that appears to the batter as a fastball until it reaches the plate, then breaks sharply on a level plane.

"Patience, Dad," Ruby urged with her hand cupped around her mouth. However, she knew her father couldn't hear her over the din of the crowd.

Still, Guy did show a little patience, laying off the third offering, a pitch in the dirt. But on the next pitch, he swung wildly at an inside curveball. He'd struck out to start the match.

The cranks cheered as the home team

whipped the ball around the infield. Those rooters who had presented coupons at the box office—which looked like virtually everyone in attendance—waved their flags.

Even though Guy had fanned leading off the first frame, he returned to the dugout with his head held high.

FAN (*v.*):
to strike out.

FRAME:
inning.

"I'll get him next time," he told his family. He then removed his cap and looked at Tales on his way to the dish. "Start us off, Old Rough and Ready."

Graham jumped up, ruffled his father's hair, and offered words of encouragement. "Shake it off, Dad," he said. "The first time I faced Cy Young, he made me look silly, but after that, I *owned* him."

Unfortunately, Tales didn't start the Travelin' Nine off. He bounced a bug bruiser to Hughie Jennings at short for the second out. Woody followed with a sky ball to Wee Willie Keeler in right garden for the last out of the first frame.

With Guy Payne as his battery mate, Preacher Wil took the hill for the bottom half of the first inning, focused solely on the task at hand. It mattered little to the hurler that the crowd was cheering louder than ever for the hometown squad, and that the dark-suited men around the Chancellor were also on their feet and applauding. Preacher Wil even appeared oblivious to the fact that the Chancellor was holding the

BUG BRUISER: *ground ball. Also called "grass clipper" (see page 169), "daisy cutter" (see page 171), or "worm burner" (see page 174).*

SKY BALL: *fly ball to the outfield, or outer garden. Also sometimes referred to as "star chaser" (see page 211) or "cloud hunter" (see page 236).*

BATTERY: *term referring to the pitcher and catcher combination.*

baseball out in the direction of home plate.

Upon finishing his warm-ups, Preacher Wil checked to make sure his fielders were ready. He waited for each one to tip his cap. Out in left garden, Elizabeth tipped hers last. Finally the hurler toed the rubber.

Wee Willie Keeler batted first for the Orioles. The scrappy right scout was the best leadoff hitter the game had ever seen. He also happened to be a top-notch bunter, and he bunted Preacher Wil's first two offerings into the cranks behind home dish.

"He did that on purpose," Griffith told his brother and sister. "He likes to bunt off pitches to get a feel for the hurler."

After taking an inside fastball for ball one, Keeler did what he did better than anyone else. He pounded the pill into the ground—a Baltimore Chop that bounced high into the air between Bubbles and Doc, and got him an infield single.

"He hit 'em where they ain't," Griffith

RUBBER: *pitching strip on the mound. The pitcher must have one foot touching the rubber when pitching.*

BUNTER: *batter who hits the ball softly and short, often to advance a runner.*

said, shaking his head. "Just like always."

Hughie Jennings, the Bombers' short-stop, batted second, and he continued with the Baltimore brand of baseball. He passed on Preacher Wil's first two pitches and then grounded a seeing-eye base hit into the hole between the Professor and Tales. Since Wee Willie Keeler had been off with the pitch, the perfectly executed hit-and-run put runners on the corners with nobody out.

Against the next hitter, Preacher Wil settled down and recorded his first strikeout of the afternoon. However, runners remained on first and third with the great John McGraw strutting to the line.

McGraw jumped on the first pitch he saw from Preacher Wil.

Crack!

The Bombers' third sack man launched a tremendous drive to left garden. Elizabeth took only one step in the direction of the

SEEING-EYE BASE HIT: *a ball that lands safely just beyond two or more fielders, so perfectly placed it's almost as if the ball has eyes, enabling the hitter to reach first base safely.*

HOLE: *space between two infielders.*

RUNNERS ON THE CORNERS: *When base runners occupy both first base and third base, a team is said to have runners on the corners.*

blast before realizing that the prodigious shot would sail deep into the bleachers.

A three-run round-tripper!

The cranks erupted. A sea of red, white, and blue flags waved about as McGraw circled the sacks.

Guy Payne didn't wait for McGraw to touch home plate before heading to the hill to talk to his hurler.

"I know exactly what my Dad's telling him," Graham said to Josiah and Happy on the bench behind him. "He's telling Preacher Wil to relax and shake it off, and that there's a lot of baseball left to be played."

"Indeed there is, Mr. Graham," Josiah agreed.

Yet when the action resumed, things didn't go much better for Preacher Wil; however, the Travelin' Nine's hurler wasn't to blame. Wilbert Robinson grounded an easy grass clipper to first, but the Professor must

ROUND-TRIPPER: *home run.* Also called *"four-bagger"* (see page 159).

GRASS CLIPPER: *ground ball.* Also called *"bug bruiser"* (see page 166), *"daisy cutter"* (see page 171), or *"worm burner"* (see page 174).

have been watching the ball with his patch as opposed to his eye, because the rock squirted through his legs and into right garden. By the time Woody chased down the pill, Robinson stood at second.

ROCK: baseball. Also called "pill" (see page 122) or "rawhide."

RAWHIDE: baseball. Also called "pill" (see page 122) or "rock."

DUCKS ON THE POND: runners on base. The ducks refer to the runners; the pond refers to the field.

Copying Wee Willie Keeler's approach, the next striker swung down and hard. His Baltimore Chop headed right for Doc, who of course had to wait for the ball to come back to earth. After fielding the rawhide, instead of firing to first right away, Doc checked the runner at second to make sure he wasn't crossing over to third. The split-second hesitation proved costly. The batter beat Doc's throw across the diamond, and once again, the Bombers had two ducks on the pond with only one man out.

Behind the home-team dugout, the Chancellor's goons stomped their feet and waved their souvenir flags like the other rooters. The Chancellor himself was equally

pleased. With a satisfied smile on his face, he
continued to massage the baseball.

"Settle down, boys!" Griffith called to the
Rough Riders.

"Let's turn two," Graham shouted.

But instead of the Travelin' Nine turning two, the Bombers *plated* two. The next
Baltimore striker lined a rope down the
right garden line. Woody cut off the bounding ball before it reached the corner, but
by the time he fired the pill back into the
infield, the hitter had cruised into second
with a stand-up double.

Once again, Guy Payne headed to the hill
to talk to his hurler. This time the Professor
and Bubbles joined the mound meeting, and
whatever was discussed seemed to work.
The next hitter grounded a daisy cutter to
second. Tales recorded the out, though the
base runner crossed over to third. But that
was as far as he got. Preacher Wil fanned

PLATE (*v.*):
*to score a run,
or tally.*

ROPE:
*hard throw or
batted ball.*

DAISY CUTTER:
*ground ball.
Also called "bug
bruiser" (see
page 166), "grass
clipper" (see page
169), or "worm
burner." (see
page 174).*

the Baltimore pitcher to finally end the frame.

Shell-shocked, the Travelin' Nine returned to the dugout. The Bombers had sent all nine men to the dish and plated five tallies. It was the most runs the Travelin' Nine had ever allowed in a single inning.

Of course the rooters, the Chancellor's entourage, and the Chancellor continued to savor the uprising. From his seat behind the hometown dugout, the Chancellor pointed the baseball one by one at the local ballists as they took their positions to start the second frame. The Chancellor appeared to believe he had something (everything) to do with what was taking place on the pitch.

"Shake it off!" Happy urged his teammates, repeating Graham's words from the top of the frame. "I don't want to see a single head hanging low. We've got eight innings to go."

TALLIES: *runs scored. On some fields, whenever the home team scored, a tally bell would sound. The tally keeper was the official scorer or scorekeeper.*

Graham laughed. "Couldn't have said it better myself," he said. He stepped to the front of the dugout and faced the players. "In Cuba, the Rough Riders rallied around the call 'Remember the *Maine!*' Well, I say, 'Remember Chicago!' We scored more than twenty runs that afternoon in the Windy City. The Travelin' Nine are capable of big innings too!"

"Huzzah!" Woody and Doc said simultaneously.

However, the barnstormers failed to score in the top of the second, though they did manage their first hit. Doc bounced a one-out single up the middle. But one pitch later, he was erased when the Professor grounded into an around-the-horn, inning-ending double play.

As the Rough Riders retook the field, Griffith, Ruby, and Graham looked at one another. They knew not to doubt the

AROUND THE HORN: *throwing the baseball around the infield.*

Travelin' Nine, but the match's unfortunate start made it difficult. Without their baseball in their hands, would there be any magic? Could there be?

In the bottom of the frame, the barnstormers were once again tight in the field. After Wee Willie Keeler hit a sky ball to Scribe for the first out, Hughie Jennings grounded a routine worm burner to Bubbles. However, the shortstop's throw to the Professor sailed high and wide, landing in the stands among the Chancellor's thugs, who ducked and scattered.

WORM BURNER: *ground ball. Also called "bug bruiser" (see page 166), "grass clipper" (see page 169), or "daisy cutter" (see page 171).*

"Do you think he did that on purpose?" Ruby asked.

"No way," Griffith replied instantly. "Bubbles would never allow a runner to reach base like that intentionally."

Fortunately, the Bombers left their teammate stranded. Preacher Wil retired the next two strikers on easy pop-ups, escaping the inning without yielding a tally.

The Travelin' Nine bats remained silent in the top of the third. Bubbles struck out, Preacher Wil lined to Hughie Jennings at short, who made a leaping one-hand grab, and Elizabeth was caught looking. A one-two-three inning.

Preacher Wil hoped to have an equally easy time in the bottom half of the frame, but Wilbert Robinson had other aspirations. Leading off the inning, he swung mightily at Preacher Wil's letter-high fastball.

Crack!

The Bombers' backstop made contact with the sweet spot on his timber. He laced a liner to left garden, a frozen rope that never rose more than ten feet off the turf. He'd smacked the rawhide so hard that when it finally reached the outfield fence, it became lodged in the wood of the wall.

Robinson's round-tripper extended the

CAUGHT LOOKING: *batter who does not swing at the third strike.*

LETTER-HIGH: *the top portion of the strike zone, usually in line with the lettering on a player's uniform.*

LINER: *line-drive batted ball.*

FROZEN ROPE: *hard line drive or throw.*

Bombers' lead. Baltimore was now ahead 6–0, and even though the home team didn't score again in the frame, that was of little consolation to Griffith, Ruby, and Graham.

	1	2	3	4	5	6	7	8	9	R
T_N	0	0	0							0
B_{OM}	5	0	1							6

14

★

Glaring Rockets, Bursting Bombs, and Gleaming Twilights

here hasn't been any magic,"
Graham said, slapping his sides.

Ruby pointed across the diamond. "He's glowing over there,"
she said, eyeing the Chancellor. "He thinks
he's in total control."

As Guy prepared to lead off the barnstormers' half of the fourth frame, Griffith
felt his frown. Despite everyone's exhorta-
tions that there was a lot of baseball left to be
played, an unease had crept into the visitors'
dugout.

Griffith peered down the bench at Preacher Wil. The hurler sat with Truman, gently stroking the hound's back. Except for the first frame and the lone mistake he'd made to Wilbert Robinson in the third, the hurler was holding his own, matching the opposing southpaw almost batter for batter.

But the barnstormers were yet to perform at the top of their game.

SET THE TABLE: *get on base.*

"This is the inning," Griffith said to his brother and sister as their father settled in at the dish.

"I hope you're right," Graham said.

Griffith smiled. "You and me—"

Crack!

Before Griffith could finish the sentence, Guy lined a clean single into left. The Travelin' Nine had their leadoff base runner on.

"Way to set the table, Dad!" Ruby cheered.

Guy pumped his fists in the direction of

the Rough Riders and then pointed to Tales digging in at the dish.

The Travelin' Nine were down six runs. Griffith wondered what strategy Tales would employ. Would he try to advance Guy into scoring position? Would he take a page from the Bombers' playbook and try the hit-and-run? Or would he take a couple of pitches and give Guy the opportunity to steal?

Tales didn't take any of those approaches. After passing up the first pitch, he lifted a sky ball to center for the first out of the frame. Woody followed that with a check-swing daisy cutter down to John McGraw at third. Since the ball was hit softly, McGraw's only play was to second, where he forced out Guy. Once again, hopes of a Rough Riders rally began to fade.

With Scribe stepping to the plate, Ruby waved her mother and father over. Since Elizabeth wasn't up for a while, and since

SCORING POSITION: *Any time a runner is on second or third bag, he is considered to be in scoring position.*

CHECK SWING: *when a batter starts to swing for the ball, but stops shortly before the ball reaches home plate.*

FORCED OUT(v.): *an out created when a runner is forced to advance because there is another runner behind him.*

Guy had just returned to the dugout, she wanted her whole family together.

"Let's all join hands," she said. "We have to keep trying different things. Something's going to work eventually. I'm sure of it."

For the first time during a game, all five Paynes joined hands—one on top of the other—without the baseball, of course.

"Positive thoughts," Graham said to his mother and father.

Guy Payne nodded.

"Focus solely on the game," Ruby added. "Don't let anything distract you."

Griffith waved Truman over too. The hound raised his paw and placed it on top of Graham's hand. There was no doubt in Griffith's mind that Truman had become part of the Payne family. The hound may have originally chosen to be with Preacher Wil, but now he was offering his unconditional love to them as well.

"Be together," Griffith whispered.

"Always," Ruby and Graham chimed in.

Suddenly a soft breeze began to blow. Crisp and clean, the gentle gust whooshed in from both left and right garden. Yet the alternating Maryland and American flags that flanked the stadium hung motionless. So did the three pennants on the center-field flagpole. The only flag paying mind to the breeze was the large Old Glory on that center-garden pole. It waved high and proud, as if something more than just that wind was causing it to stand at attention.

Griffith and Ruby peered across the diamond at the Chancellor. For the first time all afternoon, his face wasn't aglow. His satisfied smirk had been replaced by a look of concern.

"It's working," Ruby whispered as Scribe waited at the line for the first pitch.

"It sure is," said Griffith.

Scribe took the initial offering, a curveball, for strike one. He took the second pitch too, another off-speed pitch, but this one was a ball low and away. Digging his boots in a little deeper, Scribe waited for the third pitch. He cocked his bat and swung.

OFF-SPEED PITCH: *any pitch not a fastball.*

CLEANUP STRIKER: *player who hits fourth in the batting order.*

Crack!

The rawhide exploded off the cleanup striker's timber. Soaring high, the ball changed shape and color until it was a rocket glaring through the sky. Sailing toward the deepest part of center garden, it cut a red path along the blue ceiling and pierced the puffy white clouds. The ball—rocket—finally came to rest beyond the cranks in center garden.

"Home run!" Graham cheered.

"Here come the Rough Riders!" Guy exclaimed. "Six to two! We're right back in it!"

All the barnstormers had watched the ball shape-shift and soar farther than a ball could travel. As for the locals, they'd seen the ball fly a great distance, though none saw it change form.

When Scribe crossed home plate, Griffith looked over at the Chancellor. With his two scaly hands, he gripped the baseball in front of his face, a face wrinkled with a perturbed expression. Clearly, he was aware that things had changed. He probably hadn't seen the baseball turn into a rocket, but he knew that something beyond his control was taking place. And making things worse was the Travelin' Nine's exuberant celebrating, not unlike back in New Orleans.

"I got to see the magic!" Guy cheered.

"It happened even though *he* has our baseball." Graham fired a glare in the Chancellor's direction.

"I know what the magic meant!" Ruby announced.

The Travelin' Nine huddled around. Even Doc, who was batting next, returned to the dugout from the on-deck area to hear her explanation.

ON-DECK AREA: *place on the field between the dugout and home plate where the next scheduled hitter awaits his turn to bat.*

"Do tell, Miss Ruby," said Josiah. "We saw the rocket and the red glare. What did it mean?"

Ruby smiled. "It's connected to 'The Star-Spangled Banner.' The magic this afternoon is going to have to do with our national anthem. I'm sure of it!"

"I think Ruby may be right," Griffith agreed. "Maybe the magic is . . . perhaps we can use the song to help us."

Ruby looked at her older brother. "But do you think we'll be able to without our baseball?"

"I do!" Graham answered first. He pointed at the Chancellor. "He may have something that doesn't belong to him, but he can never take away *this*." He motioned to the group. "*We* are more powerful than anything he could ever have in his possession."

Excitement among the Rough Riders continued to grow when Doc and the Professor worked out back-to-back walks. With one whip of the willow, Bubbles, the next striker, could wipe away most of the deficit. But the Bombers' hurler, who appeared to be on the verge of a breakdown, managed to get the barnstormers' shortstop to ground to third, where John McGraw stepped on the sack for the force play and the final out of the frame.

WHIP OF THE WILLOW: *swing of the bat.*

• • •

Even though the Baltimore pitcher made quick work of Bubbles, the Travelin' Nine took the field in the fourth with renewed optimism. Without a doubt, the momentum had started to shift.

As Preacher Wil took the hill, Griffith, Ruby, and Graham once again huddled close. With the Rough Riders in the field, they were joined on the bench by the remaining barnstormers—Josiah, Happy, and Truman. They all locked hands (and paw, of course).

Preacher Wil's toe touched the rubber at the exact same moment that Truman's paw touched human hands. Suddenly the fair-weather clouds that had been present all day started moving about, gliding into unusual patterns. Even as the players out in the field focused on the action, they couldn't help but notice what was happening overhead. The puffy white clouds weren't moving in sync or blowing with the wind. Rather, they seemed to have minds of their own.

While the cranks may have been oblivious to the strange movements above, they were certainly aware that the sun had ducked behind the clouds, and a shadow had been cast across the park, bisecting the diamond between home plate and the hill.

"That's just like the shadow that formed on the field in Cincinnati." Ruby pointed.

"You remember the shadows?" Graham ogled his sister sideways, as she often eyed him.

"How could I forget?" she replied as Preacher Wil prepared to face his first batter. "Those shadows appeared right before the switching signal."

Griffith nodded. "The contrast between the dark and the glare makes it hard for the batter to follow the ball as—"

"Wait!" Ruby cut him off. She held up

both hands, closed her eyes, and murmured to herself.

"What are you doing?" Graham asked.

She waved her hands again, eyes still closed and lips continuing to move. Then she began to smile.

"Start singing the national anthem," she said, opening her eyes and facing her brothers.

"Why?" asked Graham.

But Griffith realized there wasn't time for questions. As Preacher Wil delivered his first pitch, he sang the first line.

"Oh, say, can you see . . ."

The ball left Preacher Wil's hand just as Griffith sang the last words. At the same moment, the sun peeked out from behind the clouds, and the shadows on the field shifted. Distracted, the striker checked his swing and tapped a comebacker to Preacher Wil. The hurler gloved the easy grass clipper and threw to Doc.

One hand dead.

COMEBACKER:
ground ball hit directly to the pitcher.

GLOVE (v.):
to field.

"You call that singing?" Graham asked, laughing at his brother.

"Well, it worked," said Griffith. He shook a playful fist.

Ruby nodded. "By using the words to 'The Star-Spangled Banner,' we can help Preacher Wil."

"I'm pretty sure you're right." Griffith beamed. "Nice work, Ruby! The strange events are going to follow the lyrics."

"If you ask me," Graham said, still chuckling, "I think it was Griff's awful singing that distracted the hitter. He probably had to cover his ears!"

Griffith growled. "Grams, if Josiah and Happy weren't standing right next—"

"Is this how things have been working all along, Mr. Griffith?" Josiah asked, stepping between the bickering brothers. "Has it been like this during the other matches?" Skepticism filled his question.

"Well, you saw how the magic worked in

HAND DEAD: *an out. ONE HAND DEAD meant "one out," TWO HANDS DEAD meant "two outs," and THREE HANDS DEAD (or DOWN) meant "three outs."*

New Orleans," answered Griffith. "Often the connection between what we're doing and what happens on the field seems like a stretch. It barely seems logical. But yes, when we're working together, this is exactly how it's been."

Griffith could tell Josiah wasn't completely convinced. Were they really causing what was happening on the field? Or was it a coincidence? At times Griffith, Ruby, and Graham hadn't been 100 percent sure either.

BUMP: *pitcher's mound. Also called "hill" (see page 122).*

Back on the bump, Preacher Wil was getting ready to face the next Baltimore batter. As soon as the Travelin' Nine's hurler delivered his pitch, Griffith and Ruby sang the first line again.

"Oh, say, can you see . . ."

This time the striker took the pitch for ball one.

"Let's add the next phrase," Ruby suggested. They waited for Preacher Wil to rock into his windup before singing.

"Oh, say, can you see by the dawn's early light . . ."

When they uttered the last two words, sunlight peeked through the gaps between the panels of the outfield fence. It came from the horizon line, at the same angle as the first streaks of sun at dawn. But was the light really from the sun? Was it a reflection? Was it something else?

The mysterious light distracted Wee Willie Keeler, who, like the first hitter of the frame, checked his swing and popped up meekly behind the plate. Guy turned around and tossed his mask. He only had to take two steps, and while standing shoulder to shoulder with the umpire, he easily caught the rock.

Two hands dead.

"One more batter to go!" Ruby exclaimed.

"This has nothing to do with magic!" roared Graham. He pointed at his brother. "This has everything to do with your dreadful singing. The hitters are trying to save their hearing!"

Griffith playfully swatted the back of Graham's head. "Little brother, you're singing with us for this batter."

"Fine," Graham said, placing a hand over his chest. "I'll show you how to carry a tune." He faced Ruby. "What's the next line?"

She eyed him sideways. "You don't know the words to 'The Star-Spangled Banner'?"

"I do, but—but—"

"Don't let Dad know," Ruby warned.

"I'll sing." Griffith groaned as Hughie Jennings waited at the dish.

"What so proudly we hailed at the twilight's last gleaming?"

Once again the clouds shifted. This time the field appeared as it would at dusk, even though it was hours before early evening.

"Keep it up, Griff!" Graham cheered, hiding his smirk with his hand. "Now your singing is scaring the clouds!"

It remained dark for the entire at bat. Each time Preacher Wil threw the ball, Ruby and Graham recited the line along with Griffith. Unable to see any of the pitches, the striker didn't even bother swinging. What was the use? He was called out on strikes, and for the first time all afternoon, Preacher Wil had retired the side in order.

Three hands dead!

RETIRED THE SIDE: *when the pitcher or defensive team has recorded the three outs in an inning.*

Preacher Wil struck out to lead off the fifth frame, but the Travelin' Nine weren't concerned. The barnstormers preferred that their hurler rest between innings as opposed to expending energy running the bases. The team wanted him to be fresh on the bump.

Consequently, Happy encouraged the next strikers to take their time getting to and from home plate, just in case this happened to be a quick frame.

"This isn't going to be a quick inning," Elizabeth assured Happy.

"I second that," said Guy.

The three Payne kids gathered on the top step of the dugout. For the first time, their parents would be batting one right after the other in the same frame.

At the dish, Elizabeth waited for a strike before swinging. Then she surprised everyone in Union Park by bunting. Obviously she'd been studying Tales and Bubbles or some of the local players like Hughie Jennings or Wee Willie Keeler, because her perfectly placed bunt stopped dead in the turf between the mound and third base.

The barnstormers applauded the textbook bunt base hit.

"Come on, Dad!" Graham cheered.

Like his wife before him, Guy Payne took the first pitch. The switch hitter, batting from the right side against the southpaw, was waiting for the ball to cross the dish exactly where he wanted it.

"I reckon a nice offensive explosion would be just fine about now," said Woody, grabbing his bat and stepping into the on-deck area.

"Explosions!" Ruby exclaimed.

"Bombs bursting in air!" Griffith shouted.

Crack!

Guy smoked a line drive the opposite way deep into the gap in right-center garden. Higher and higher it climbed, and then suddenly the ball seemed to *detonate* like an explosive in midair. It smashed into the outfield wall (leaving a dent and smoke), then ricocheted past Wee Willie Keeler.

"Go, Dad!" yelled Ruby.

"Run, Mom!" Graham shouted.

Elizabeth tore around the bases. By the time Keeler reached the rock, she was

SWITCH HITTER: *a player who is able to bat either right-handed or left-handed.*

GAP: *the section of the outfield between the outfielders.*

"Bombs bursting in air!"

rounding third, and by the time he fired the ball into the cutoff man, she'd crossed the dish.

Guy Payne wasn't slowing down either. It was clear to everyone in the stadium he'd set his sights on an inside-the-park home run. Running as fast as Crazy Feet ever did, he sped past the shortstop and zipped around third. The dash to the dish was on!

The Rough Riders climbed to the top step of the dugout.

The relay man whirled and fired to the catcher. It was going to be a bang-bang play at the plate.

"Go, Dad!" Ruby cried again.

"Just like Louisville!" called Griffith.

Elizabeth must have heard Griffith, and like her oldest son, she recalled that play well. Standing behind the catcher, she frantically waved her arms and signaled for her husband to slide on the outside part of the plate.

The catcher reached for the ball and

CUTOFF MAN: *infielder who catches a throw from an outfielder in an attempt to hold up a base runner who is heading for a base or home plate or to help a ball get to its intended target faster.*

INSIDE-THE-PARK HOME RUN: *a home run that does not go over the wall or leave the field of play.*

gloved the throw. Guy leaped into his slide. Both arrived at the dish at the same moment. However, the tip of Guy's boot touched the outside corner of the plate a millisecond before the catcher's mitt grazed his boot strings.

Safe!

"Home run!" Ruby cheered, bursting out of the dugout. Her brothers followed.

Even though it was the middle of the inning and on-the-field celebrations were frowned upon (and considered by most to be poor sportsmanship), the three Paynes couldn't control their joy. Griffith, Ruby, and Graham needed to congratulate their mother and father.

As a family, they returned to the dugout.

Woof! Woof! Woof! Woof!

"Four barks for four tallies!" Griffith declared, acknowledging Truman's greeting. "The dog can count!"

Graham had thought the same thing upon hearing the barks; however, he wasn't about to let Griffith know. He quickly turned away (so his older brother couldn't read his face) and spotted George in the stands. Like before, he was stuffing his face, this time with cotton candy, and of course, his grin stretched ear to ear. He was with the other boys, all of whom were cheering for the Travelin' Nine. No, they hadn't turned into fair-weather fans and abandoned their hometown allegiance. Rather, they were simply showing their appreciation for the fine exploits of the Rough Riders. Like many of the other rooters, they were behaving like *true* baseball fans.

After the hometown hurler retired Tales and Woody to end the frame, Graham headed down the dugout to get closer to George. But halfway there, he stopped. A chill surged through his limbs.

Josiah was pacing the middle step of the dugout. His chin was lowered to his chest, and he had both hands dug deeply into the pockets of his tattered pants; the fingers of his left hand could be seen sticking out of a hole in the bottom of the pocket. He was muttering to himself too.

Gazing across the diamond, Graham detected the source of Josiah's distress. The Chancellor had erupted. His face was beet red, and he was berating one of his men, whom he had by the lapel. As the Chancellor's shouting grew louder, many of his men rose from their seats, attempting to avoid being next to incur his wrath. Backing away, some stepped from the cordoned-off area and stood among the cranks.

"Get behind me," Griffith said to Graham, moving in front of his brother so that he was hidden from the Chancellor's field of vision.

Griffith also found the sight of Josiah so

distraught terribly upsetting. However, unlike his younger brother, he sensed an additional reason for Josiah's state. The Chancellor had turned desperate. Even though he held the baseball, it wasn't serving him; strange events on the pitch were working against his team. Desperate men were driven to desperate acts. There was no telling what he might try next.

Once the home half of the inning started, the Chancellor settled down some. His yelling abated, and he no longer held on to any of his men. When he returned to his seat, most of his men rejoined him in the reserved section, but they couldn't have liked what was taking place between the white lines.

BETWEEN THE WHITE LINES: *on the playing field, in fair territory.*

In that fifth frame, Preacher Wil retired the Bombers without giving up a run, and this time, instead of his fielders betraying him, they lent a hand. Against the leadoff batter, Elizabeth made a running catch heading toward the left garden line. Then

John McGraw tried bunting his way on, but Preacher Wil, showing catlike reflexes, burst from the bump, barehanded the roller, and shoveled the pill to Doc to get him by a stride. To close out the inning, Bubbles made a sliding catch behind second sack of Wilbert Robinson's sinking humpback liner.

Three up, three down.

The Travelin' Nine had set aside the Bombers in order. Of note, they'd done so without the help of the three Payne kids. Because of the Chancellor's outburst, Griffith, Ruby, and Graham had opted to hold off trying anything for a half inning (but only for a half inning). Still, the three kids knew they had the ability to generate *extraordinary* events on the pitch, even without the baseball in their possession. The power of their unity and their belief in one another was strong enough to call its magic to them.

Now, heading to the sixth, it was a brand-new ball game!

As Scribe made his way to the dish to start the frame, Ruby searched for signs, gazing around Union Park. Once again her lips were moving as she looked for something— anything—that would trigger the next clue.

"Who are you talking to?" Graham asked, smirking.

"Francis Scott Key," Ruby replied matter-of-factly.

Graham's jaw dropped.

"I'm teasing, Grams," said Ruby, rolling her eyes. "Did you really believe I was having a conversation with the composer of 'The Star-Spangled Banner'?"

Graham shrugged. "Ruby, I wouldn't put anything past you."

After Scribe hit a sky ball out to right, Ruby pointed to the flags lining the stadium and then to the large one blowing in the stiff breeze beyond center garden. "This inning is about the Stars and Stripes," she said. "Look at the shadow from the flagpole."

"It stretches all the way across left field," said Graham.

"Exactly, but that's not where it should be."

"You're right," Griffith agreed. "That shadow isn't from the sun."

"Exactly," Ruby repeated. "I have no idea what's causing it."

"That's where Doc needs to hit the ball!" Griffith and Graham said together.

"Exactly!"

Hearing his name, Doc glanced at the barnstormers' bench. The three kids pointed to the *stripe* in left garden. Doc tapped the brim of his cap, turned to the hurler, and then stroked the next offering into left field.

"Base hit!" Griffith announced.

"Here we go!" cheered Graham.

Ruby raced to the end of the dugout and jumped onto the top step. "The Stars and Stripes are going to guide us this inning," she said to the ballists as the Professor headed to the dish. "We're not exactly sure how, so just be alert."

When the Professor reached the line, more stripes appeared on the pitch, but unlike a moment ago, these *were* caused by the clouds and sun.

"Which one should he aim for?" Graham asked his sister.

Ruby looked toward home plate. Like Graham, Professor Lance was awaiting her response.

"The broad stripe!" Griffith exclaimed, pointing to the widest line on the field, which carved a path through right garden.

The Professor inched off the plate, waited for a pitch he could poke the opposite way,

and blooped a single into right. The Travelin'
Nine had two batters on.

"Now all the stripes are the same width,"
Griffith said as Bubbles settled in at the dish.

"Let's try something else." Ruby reached
for her brothers' hands and began rocking
them back and forth.

"What are we doing?" Graham asked.

But Ruby didn't need to answer. On the
pitch, the shadow-stripes had started to
move in sync with their hands, undulating
like a flag.

"What do you think this means?" Graham
asked.

"Banner yet wave!" declared Griffith.

"Yes!" Ruby triumphed. "Keep swinging."

With Bubbles at the line, the three Paynes
moved their hands to and fro. In turn, the
stripes on the green oasis continued to
mimic their motion. Bubbles worked the
count full and then bounced a bug bruiser

toward the left side of the infield. The rock zigzagged across the diamond toward third sack, bounded toward the bump, and then shot toward shortstop. The hapless fielders could barely follow the ball, let alone glove a pill that moved in impossible-to-anticipate directions. Riding the waving stripes, the rawhide rolled into left garden for a roundabout base hit, and even though Doc could have scored from second, he chose not to chance it with only one out.

"Now that's what I call hitting it where they ain't!" Griffith proclaimed.

While the cranks didn't know what was really happening, they knew exactly what was happening. The visiting team had the makings of a big rally. With one gone, the Travelin' Nine had three ducks on the pond.

Up stepped Preacher Wil.

Woof! Woof! Woof! Woof!

"Four barks for four tallies!" Graham announced before Griffith could.

"I like the way that sounds," said Griffith, beaming. "Now which lines from 'The Star-Spangled Banner' might sound like a home run? Because I'd sure love to see Preacher Wil—"

"Gallantly streaming!" Ruby blurted. "Let's sing that whole bar."

GRAND SLAM: *home run that is hit with the bases loaded.*

Without hesitation, the three children recited the verse:

"Whose broad stripes and bright stars, through the perilous fight, O'er the ramparts we watch'd, were so gallantly streaming?"

Preacher Will swung with all his might.

Ka-boom!

The majestic blast streamed across the sky and soared past the flag in center garden.

"Grand slam!" Graham shouted, raising both arms high overhead.

With one whip of the willow, the two-run deficit had become a two-run lead. The Travelin' Nine now led by a score of 8–6.

The barnstormers greeted Preacher Wil when he reached the dugout with hand-shakes, hugs, and licks (though only Truman did the licking).

"Keep this rally going!" Happy cheered.

"What should we try now?" Graham turned to Ruby.

She thought for a moment. "Let's go back to what we did when Bubbles was up."

With Elizabeth digging her boots in at the dish, the three Paynes joined hands again. This time, however, their swinging arms had a far different effect. They placed the hometown fielders on unsteady ground; they could barely remain upright. But because they couldn't see the undulating stripes, the Bombers had no idea why they suddenly were unable to keep their balance. As they struggled to stand, Elizabeth grounded a daisy cutter that hopped over a toppling John McGraw at third sack. The ball bounded into left for a double.

"Way to go, Mom!" Griffith pumped a fist.

"Keep it going, Dad!" cheered Ruby as Guy Payne stepped from the on-deck area.

Suddenly Josiah pointed to the outfield. The eagle sat perched atop the center garden flagpole. He had one wing extended, pointing to stars. Amazingly, in the middle of the afternoon, stars appeared in the blue sky, like the stars in the blue canton of the American flag.

"Proof through the night!" Griffith and Ruby declared.

"Like the flag," Graham added, "we're always going to be there."

Guy Payne looked back at his children. He didn't have to be told what needed to be done. As darkness fell across the field, he aimed for the stars.

Boom!

On the first pitch, he blasted his second home run of the afternoon, though this one wasn't an inside-the-park round tripper. This one was a no-doubt-about-it four-bagger.

"That's what I call a star chaser!" Griffith cheered.

The Travelin' Nine now led 10–6. The match was indeed a whole new ball game.

STAR CHASER: *fly ball to the outfield, or outer garden. Also sometimes referred to as a "sky ball" (see page 166), or "cloud hunter" (see page 236).*

15

★

By George

ey, Graham."

Graham peered over the top of the dugout.

George was bounding down the aisle toward the field as the Travelin' Nine took the pitch to start the seventh frame. However, this time, George wasn't with the other boys. Nor was he eating. But of course he was smiling, and his smile right now contained a hint of mischievousness.

"Hi, George," Graham said, waving.

Without asking permission or hesitating, George hopped the fence.

"I'm spending an inning on the bench," he announced, standing on the field next to the visitors' dugout.

Graham was pretty sure George wasn't permitted in the dugout during the match, but he wasn't about to tell him he couldn't stay. Glancing down the bench, Graham saw that Josiah and Happy didn't seem to mind his presence.

"You enjoying the match?" Graham asked, leading George into the dugout.

"Oh, yeah," he said, sitting down on the top step. He waved to Josiah and Happy at the far end. "A lot more than I thought I would. One day I'm going to play baseball in a stadium like this and smack four-baggers farther than everyone."

"Maybe you will," said Graham, beaming at the big little boy as they moved to the bench. He still found it hard to believe he was nearly twice as old as George.

"Who's he?" George pointed to Truman.

"One day I'm going to play baseball in a stadium like this."

The hound walked gingerly over, sat down at the bottom of the steps in front of George, and stared up at the visitor.

"He's Preacher Wil's dog." Graham nodded in the direction of the hurler facing his first batter in the bottom of the sixth. "His name is Truman."

George leaned forward and patted the hound on the head. Then he peeked over his shoulder. "These are some good seats," he said with a grin. "I could get used to watching a match from in here."

Graham glanced down the bench at his siblings, intently following the action. After each pitch, either Griffith or Ruby looked his way. Graham knew they'd prefer him to sit with them, since there couldn't be any strange events unless they were together. But they'd held off trying to make the magic happen in the bottom of the fifth, so Graham didn't figure it would be a problem.

If Griffith and Ruby needed him—if things started taking a wrong turn—he could easily join them. Right now, Graham needed to be with George. He wasn't exactly sure why, he just knew that he did.

On the field, Preacher Wil quickly disposed of the leadoff hitter, fanning him on four pitches.

"I'm a southpaw too," George said, pointing to Preacher Wil and then tapping his left arm. "That means I throw lefty."

"I know," said Graham, matching his new friend's grin. "My dad taught me that term."

"I'd love to be able to pitch like that," George added. "Hit farther and pitch faster." His smile turned sheepish, and he lowered his voice. "But first I need to figure out how to hit a target. I'm a little on the wild side."

With Preacher Wil having easily retired the first batter, Griffith and Ruby had stopped glancing Graham's way after every pitch. As in the previous inning, the Travelin' Nine were proving they were more than capable of holding their own against the Bombers.

"I liked watching him bat," George said, motioning to Woody in right garden. "I think he's your best hitter."

"He's one of the best," said Graham. "He's also got a great glove and a rifle arm." Then he added, "That's my dad behind the dish, and my mom out in left garden."

But at the moment, George wasn't the least bit interested in Graham's parents. "Look at the size of him!" he exclaimed, pointing to the Travelin' Nine's center scout.

RIFLE (*ADJ.*): *hard-throwing.*

"That's Scribe," Graham said. "He's our biggest bopper."

"Look at the size of me!" George jumped to his feet on the bench, nearly clocking his head on the top of the dugout. He laughed, thumped his chest, and plopped back down. "If I keep growing like this, that's what I'm going to look like when I get older."

Graham smiled wider than ever. He loved talking baseball with his not-so-little friend.

Sitting shoulder to shoulder, Graham and George watched as Preacher Wil took care of the next two strikers, retiring both on daisy cutters to Doc. On each play, Preacher Wil broke from the bump as soon as the ball was hit to the right side. He caught the first bag man's flips to him in stride.

ONE-TWO-THREE FRAME: *when the pitcher retires all three batters he faces in an inning in order.*

A third consecutive one-two-three frame for Preacher Wil.

After the final out, Guy was first to the dugout. He headed straight for Graham and George.

"I see you've made yourself a friend," Guy said.

"This is George," said Graham.

Guy shook the boy's hand. "Nice to meet you."

"Nice to meet you, too, sir," George said,

staring at his catcher's gear. "I've never seen equipment like that before." He stood up so that he could touch the padding over Guy's chest and get a closer look at the leather mask resting on top of his head.

"You're a baseball fan, son?" Guy asked.

"I am now," replied George, pumping a fist toward the pitch. "Thanks to Graham. But I have to say, I like playing the game more than watching it."

Guy smiled. "Most people do."

"He's the reason I came down to the dugout," George said to Guy. He pointed across the field toward the Chancellor.

Graham froze.

"Why?" Guy asked. The color drained from his face. "What did he do?"

"Last inning, I heard him talking. I was—"

"Why didn't you say something to me?" Graham interrupted.

George shrugged. "You're just a kid,"

he replied. He motioned with his thumb to Josiah and Happy. "I was going to say something to them, but when I got here, I couldn't believe how close I was to the action. Then we started talking about baseball, and I totally forgot why I came here in the first place." He shrugged again. "I get distracted easily."

"I know what you mean." Graham chuckled. "Me too."

"Son, what did you hear?" Guy asked, placing his hand on George's back.

"I didn't mean to listen to their conversation. I heard them talking when I passed by on the way back from the concession stand."

"What did he say?" Guy pressed.

George paused. "Something about not caring about money or what happens in this match. He kept saying he was going to defeat you anyway. He said it over and over, whatever that means."

"Son, you did the right thing by coming to us." Guy patted George's back and then glanced at the Rough Riders who'd gathered around.

"He mentioned you by name." George pointed to Graham. "How does he know you?"

Graham didn't answer. He scrunched his face into a knot, clenched his fists, and turned toward the Chancellor.

"What did he say about Graham?" Guy asked George, moving his hand onto the boy's shoulder.

George paused again. "That he's going to get him one way or the other, just like he got some baseball. Something like that, I think."

Graham still didn't avert his eyes, unclench his fists, or relax his face. Even when George told him he was heading back into the stands because he wanted to be with his friends for the seventh-inning stretch, Graham couldn't look away. All he could do was tremble and stare.

The Bombers set aside the Travelin' Nine without giving up a tally in the top of the seventh, but across the field, the Chancellor hardly seemed pleased. His satisfied smile, a fixture on his face those first few innings, was now a distant memory. The hometown club continued to trail.

Graham watched as the Chancellor ordered his men to gather around. Clutching the baseball in his left hand, the Chancellor jerked his head, waved his free arm, and then stabbed the air with his index finger. Then the Chancellor addressed a few of his men individually and others in groups of two or three.

Graham's trembling turned to shaking. He'd never been more frightened. Not when the magic first appeared back in Cincinnati.

Not when Griffith leaped off the train in Minneapolis. Not when the thugs attacked them in New Orleans.

Never.

	1	2	3	4	5	6	7	8	9	R
T N	0	0	0	2	2	6	0			10
B O M	5	0	1	0	0	0				6

16

★

A Pause in the Action

adies and gentle-men," the umpire bellowed into a megaphone from atop the pitcher's mound. "May I have your attention, please?"

As the Travelin' Nine began taking the field for the home half of the seventh, the umpire requested they line up along the third base line. Escorting them over, he informed the Rough Riders that a special seventh-inning stretch ceremony would be held.

At first Griffith was suspicious, thinking this could be another one of the Chancellor's devious schemes. However, the umpire's demeanor and the joyous expressions on the faces of the hometown ballists told him otherwise.

The umpire waited for the din of the cranks to subside, but even with the megaphone, there was no way the thousands in attendance would be able to hear his words.

"This afternoon we celebrate Fort McHenry, Francis Scott Key, and the seventy-fifth anniversary of 'The Star-Spangled Banner.'" He waved to the area in back of home plate. "At this time, it is my distinguished pleasure to introduce to you this charming city's new mayor, the Honorable Thomas G. Hayes, and the governor of the great state of Maryland, the Honorable Lloyd Lowndes Jr."

As the two local officials stepped foot

on the green oasis, a brass band, which had assembled in center garden, played a welcome march. The cranks clapped and stomped while the dignitaries made their way to the mound.

"On this day," the umpire continued, "we also honor the brave men who have so valiantly served in our nation's armed forces." He motioned to the outer garden, where groups of men dressed in military attire were filing in. "May I introduce to you the veterans of the Mexican War." He pointed to the men marching in from right garden. He then pivoted to the larger contingent entering from behind the band in center field. "Please welcome the servicemen of the Civil War." Next he motioned to left garden, where the largest group of all was assembling. "And here are the national heroes who served our country in the war in Cuba last year." The umpire cleared his throat and waved to the barnstormers. "At this time, I now ask that the members of the Travelin' Nine join these soldiers."

As all the veterans from the different wars congregated in the outfield, the band struck up a military march. Fireworks and firecrackers whistled and popped, while the cranks cheered and waved their flags, once again turning the grandstand into a sea of red, white, and blue.

"I reckon we should head out there," Woody said to his fellow Rough Riders, still standing in a row between home dish and third sack.

So they did. But when Elizabeth and Preacher Wil remained on the foul line (because they hadn't served in Cuba), the umpire hurried over and insisted they join the soldiers. He waved Happy out of the dugout too.

This was the first time these Rough

Riders had been acknowledged and honored since their return from the war. To a man, they were deeply moved. When they reached their spots in left garden, Woody, Bubbles, and the Professor stood at attention and held their salutes. Tales placed his hand on his chest, as he would when reciting the Pledge of Allegiance. Happy and Scribe shed tears.

"Did you have any idea about this?" Guy said to Doc.

"Not a clue," he replied. "I'm as surprised as you are."

When Guy looked Graham's way, Graham stood as tall as he could and saluted him. His father saluted him back.

Once all the veterans were assembled in the outfield, the seventh-inning stretch festivities and fun commenced. A posse of clowns, all dressed as Uncle Sam, chased one another around the bases. Groups of young, uniformed schoolchildren danced in the outfield. Ushers and attendants ran along the outfield foul lines and, using slingshots, launched bags of peanuts and boxes of Cracker Jack into the crowd. Everyone in attendance savored the celebration.

FOUL LINES: *lines extending from home plate through first and third base and all the way to the outfield. Anything within the lines is considered to be in fair territory; anything outside the lines is in foul territory.*

Well, almost everyone.

The Chancellor surely had to have known there was going to be a ceremony commemorating the anniversary of the national anthem, but he was obviously blindsided by this additional tribute to the Travelin' Nine.

As the on-field entertainment delighted the rooters, Graham's eyes remained fixed on the Chancellor and his dark-suited thugs. The Chancellor was once again berating several of his men, while holding the baseball tightly with both hands.

The baseball.

229

The Chancellor was . . . berating several of his men.

The Chancellor had their baseball, and even though things were going well in the match, Graham knew the barnstormers needed to get it back. Whatever plot the Chancellor was scheming was about to be launched, and without the baseball in their possession . . .

17

★

The Final Frames

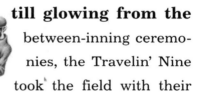

till glowing from the between-inning ceremonies, the Travelin' Nine took the field with their heads held high and an added bounce in their step.

However, the Bombers weren't quite ready to put down their gloves and surrender, even with the last man in their order leading off. The hometown club's weak-hitting pitcher dropped a beautiful bunt that rolled to a stop on the first base line—an infield hit.

Up stepped Wee Willie Keeler, and against Preacher Wil, he did what he did best. The crafty batsman Baltimore-chopped the rock straight down on home plate. By the time the ball landed in Guy's mitt, the speedster had already crossed first sack. And since Doc Lindy had charged in attempting to field the pill, the Bombers' pitcher wisely crossed all the way over to third when he saw no one covering the bag. Suddenly Baltimore had runners on the corners with nobody out.

Up stepped Hughie Jennings, and when he saw Keeler running on Preacher Wil's first offering, he opted to take the pitch. The fast-footed right scout stole second.

With men now on second and third and still no one out, Preacher Wil and Guy decided to take the bat out of Hughie Jennings's hands. In order to create a force at every base, they intentionally walked the Bombers' shortstop.

INTENTIONALLY WALK (v.): *when a pitcher deliberately throws four balls to a batter, advancing the hitter to first base.*

"Looks like Preacher Wil could use our help," Graham said as Baltimore's number three hitter made his way to the dish.

"What lines haven't we used from 'The Star-Spangled Banner'?" Griffith asked Ruby.

She thought for a moment. "We've used almost all of them."

"Not the last one," said Graham, "and these are the last innings."

Ruby smiled. "That sounds about right to me."

"'O'er the land of the free and the home of the brave'?" Griffith recited the line.

"Mr. Griffith," Josiah said, shuffling over, "I do believe you should focus on home plate."

"I was thinking the same thing." Griffith pointed to his father behind the dish. "That sure is the home of the brave."

As Preacher Wil toed the rubber, the

three Paynes joined hands, crouched down like their father, and directed their attention to the plate. Preacher Wil's first pitch was a breaking ball in the dirt. The rawhide had such movement that it completely fooled the striker, who swung anyway. Still, Guy had to block the rock with his body, and if he'd allowed the pill to skip by, one or even two runs would've scored. The next offering from the Travelin' Nine hurler was a tailing fastball. Once again, the batter flailed at the pitch, which started in the strike zone but ended up way away. Guy scooted out of his crouch and gloved the rock with his backhand, preventing another potential wild pitch. Then Preacher Wil fired a bloop curve, a pitch so high and so slow that the batter had to wait for the ball to come down and time his swing. The pill never reached the plate. It bounced on the dish as the batter swung and missed. Guy scooped up the pitch on the high hop.

BREAKING BALL: *curveball.*

TAILING FASTBALL: *a type of fastball pitch that bends downward and away from right-handed hitters.*

WILD PITCH: *a pitch so far from the strike zone that the catcher cannot catch or block it, permitting any base runner to advance.*

Sluggers

Three pitches, three swings, one man gone.

"That was the strangest at bat I ever saw," Ruby said, shaking her head, "and we've seen lots of strange at bats this summer."

"Do you think we had something to do with that?" Graham asked.

CLOUD HUNTER: *fly ball to the outfield, or outer garden. Also sometimes referred to as "sky ball" (see page 166), or "star chaser" (see page 211).*

Neither Griffith nor Ruby answered because both were already back to focusing on their father. John McGraw was at the line, and the bases were still loaded.

Like the batter before him, McGraw swung at the first pitch, but unlike the previous hitter, McGraw made contact, lifting a sky ball down the left field line.

"Go, Mom!" Ruby shouted.

While Elizabeth went chasing after the hooking cloud hunter, her cap flew off, and her long hair blew in the breeze. At the last possible instant, she lunged for the rock. Her dive appeared to defy gravity—was it because her three kids had instinctively thrown their hands forward? Free of the earth's pull, she soared through the air— like Woody when he was thrown from the horse in Louisville and Crazy Feet when he was launched by the cow's tail in Chicago. As her mitt brushed the tips of the blades of grass, Elizabeth snared the ball.

Two hands dead.

But the Bombers' pitcher was tagging up from third!

In one motion, Elizabeth skidded to a halt, popped to her feet, and using her cannonlike throwing arm, fired the rock toward home. The pea soared parallel to the turf, low and fast. It sailed by Bubbles, the cutoff man, who let the ball go, and blew through the infield. At the dish, Guy prepared for the throw and braced for impact. The Bombers' base runner was charging like a runaway train barreling down the tracks. But Guy Payne

TAG UP (v.): *to advance to the next base after a fly-ball out.*

PEA: *hard throw.*

wasn't about to give ground. Straddling the dish, he was determined to block the plate. The ball skipped into his glove on one perfect hop. The hometown ballist lowered his shoulder . . . .

Smash!

The force of the violent collision sent both ballists flying into the air. Then they crashed down on top of the dish.

The umpire leaned over the prone players. He peered inside Guy's glove. Had the Rough Rider managed to hold on to the rock?

"Out!" the umpire called, pointing to the pill in the catcher's leather. "Three hands dead!"

"Now that's what I call the home of the brave!" Josiah cheered, motioning to home plate.

As the husband and wife trotted off the field, the Travelin' Nine congratulated them for protecting the team's lead with their outstanding defensive play.

However, the barnstormers failed to add to that lead in the top half of the eighth inning. The team was set down in order.

"We've used up all the lyrics," Ruby said as Preacher Wil got set to face his first striker of the frame.

"Maybe that means the Rough Riders don't need our help anymore," Graham added.

In the eighth, Preacher Wil retired the first two batters he faced. The barnstormers were now just four outs away from victory.

But then the Travelin' Nine's hurler issued a base on balls, followed by a single to center, followed by another free pass. In the blink of an eye, the Bombers had the bases loaded again and the tying run coming to the plate in the form of Wee Willie Keeler.

As Preacher Wil prepared to pitch to the

BASE ON BALLS: *walk. If a batter receives four pitches out of the strike zone in one plate appearance, he advances to first base.*

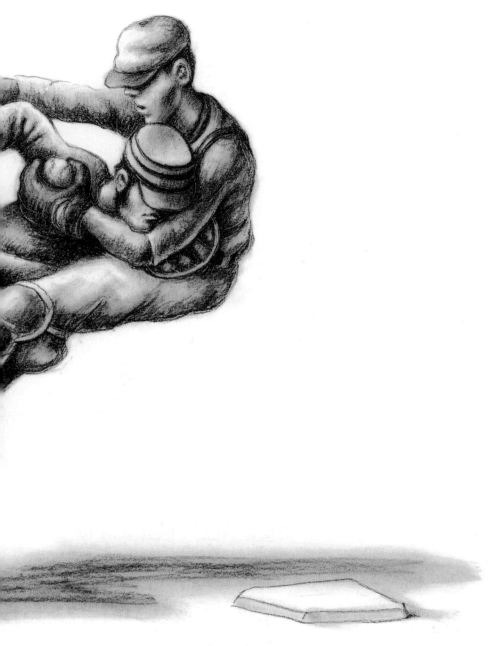

Smash!

pesky right scout, the Travelin' Nine shuffled into position. Even though Keeler was a spray hitter, the barnstormers knew he had a few spots where he liked to hit the ball more than others. Elizabeth set herself in shallow left garden and toward the line.

SPRAY HITTER: *batter who hits the ball to all fields.*

Suddenly she started sprinting toward the infield, sneaking in behind third sack. She was trying to pick off the runner leading from third!

PICK OFF: *an attempt by a pitcher or fielder to get a base runner out by throwing to the base.*

Behind home plate, Guy leaped out of his crouch and pointed Preacher Wil to third bag. Since he was a southpaw, Preacher Wil had his back to the left side of the diamond and couldn't see what was happening. But he trusted his catcher. Without looking, he lifted his rear foot from the rubber (so as to avoid being called for a balk) and flipped the ball *behind his back* toward third sack. The no-look toss was perfectly timed and placed. Ducking in behind the runner, who had

BALK: *the penalty for an illegal movement by the pitcher. The rule prevents pitchers from deliberately deceiving base runners, who advance one base if the penalty is called.*

strayed several strides off base, Elizabeth caught the ball and slapped the tag.

"Yer out!" the umpire called. "Three hands dead!"

"What a play!" Happy cheered.

"That had to be magic!" Graham declared as the triumphant Travelin' Nine raced off the green oasis.

"No way," said Griffith, raising a fist high. "That's just baseball like it oughta be!"

For the Chancellor, the pick-off play was the last straw. Before all the Rough Riders reached the dugout, he'd stormed up the aisle and out of Union Park.

The final inning of the game didn't have much drama, if any. With the home team trailing by four, everyone in the stadium knew what the outcome would be. Still, the rooters remained. The cranks had come out

for an anniversary celebration and an entertaining baseball match—and entertaining it
had been, even if their team was losing.

The Rough Riders didn't score in their half
of the ninth, and even though Preacher Wil
had to face the top of the Bombers' order in
the bottom of the last, he wasn't concerned.
Nor were the barnstormers.

In the bottom of the ninth, the first two
strikers skied to Scribe in center garden,
while the final batter grounded to Tales, who
flipped to Professor Lance for the final out of
the frame.

The ball game was over. The Travelin'
Nine had won, 10–6.

As the barnstormers gathered around home
plate to congratulate one another on their
hard-fought victory, the Baltimore Bombers stood on the top step of their dugout and
applauded the opposing team. After several

SKY (v.):
to hit a fly ball.

minutes, the Bombers lined up and marched back onto the green oasis. Led by Guy, the Travelin' Nine fell into formation as well. The two lines strode toward each other so the players could exchange handshakes.

But before Guy Payne reached the first ballist, Griffith charged in front of his father, a look of terror on his face.

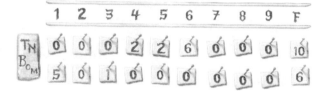

18

★

Josiah and Happy

"**h e r e ' s**
H a p p y ? "
Griffith asked.

Ruby raced up
alongside him. "Where's Josiah?"

Neither man was on the field for the post-game celebration.

Woof! Woof!

Truman bolted toward the dugout. The barnstormers and many of the Bombers followed the dog and watched as Truman sniffed the area where Happy and Josiah had been sitting. Growling, the hound appeared to detect a scent. At the end of the dugout, he walked up the steps and back onto the pitch, stopping by the fence where the field met the bleachers.

Woof! Woof!

On the ground was a Travelin' Nine cap. Truman picked it up in his mouth and brought it over to Griffith.

"This is Happy's," Griffith said, his voice quivering.

"What happened to Josiah and Happy?" Ruby asked, looking at the cap in her brother's hand, her eyes fixed on the large boot print across the brim.

"Maybe he knows!" Graham pointed.

As the cranks were making their way up the aisle behind the visitor's dugout toward the exit, George charged down the bleachers, taking them two and three at a time.

Graham hurried to the fence. "Did you see the two older men who were sitting on the bench?"

"They took—took them," George panted, leaning on the fence. "The men with the suits—took them."

Graham placed a hand on his new friend's shoulder. "Where did they go?"

George looked up the aisle. "They took them," he repeated.

"We have to find them!" Griffith cried. He raced from one Rough Rider to another. "We can't just stand here."

Guy grabbed Griffith's arm. "We'll find them."

Griffith shook his head. His breaths came quickly, and his chest tightened.

"We'll find them, Griff," said Graham, stepping over to his brother and repeating his father's words. He then looked at Ruby, who had one hand over her mouth and one in her empty pocket. "We will," he said.

This was what the Chancellor had been plotting. Gazing into the stands, Graham watched as the cranks continued to make their way out of Union Park. There were still so many fans at the stadium. How were they possibly going to find Happy and Josiah?

"Son, I need you to think for a moment." Guy walked up to George, reached over the fence, and placed his hand on the boy's back. "Try to recall what you heard those men say, if anything."

George lowered his head. He was still leaning against the fence, trying to catch his breath.

"Anything at all," Graham added, joining his father. He rested his hand on George's chubby forearm.

"Anything, son," Guy pressed.

George looked up, eyes wide.

"What is it?" asked Graham.

"A boat," George murmured. "They mentioned a boat." His friends were calling to him now.

"Happy can't swim," Griffith said, walking up.

"Josiah can't either," added Woody.

Guy nodded. "The Chancellor and I met in Baltimore harbor. Chances are—"

"What's he going to do?" Griffith asked,

interrupting his father. The feelings of panic that had started to abate quickly returned.

Guy didn't answer. He watched as George ran to rejoin his friends by the stadium exit. Guy then turned back to his wife, who had hurried up to Griffith. Standing behind her older son, she hugged him tightly.

"Where are they?" Ruby asked.

"I know exactly where," said Guy. "The same place he took me. I'm sure of it."

"I don't know, Guy," the Professor said, adjusting the cord of his eye patch. "He might be setting you up. He knows you know about that place. He wants—"

"You're right," Guy interrupted. "But I have to go after them anyway."

"No," said Elizabeth, still holding on to Griffith. "You can't leave us again."

"We're all going," Doc declared. "We don't leave men behind. We didn't in Cuba. We won't in Baltimore."

"I must go alone," Guy insisted. "It's the only—"

"It's too much of a risk," said Tales. He twirled one end of his bushy mustache. "We won't let you go by yourself. We stand by you."

"Then stand by my decision," Guy said firmly. He looked from soldier to soldier. "You've always trusted me, and I ask that you trust me now. I cannot allow any of you to be placed in harm's way. The Chancellor has already killed my brother. He won't think twice about killing again. I won't allow you to place your lives—"

"What about us?" Elizabeth cut her husband off. She motioned to their children. "You can't do this to us again."

Guy stepped over to his wife and placed both his hands on her cheeks.

She bowed her head and closed her eyes.

"Look at me," Guy said gently. "Please, Liz. Look at me."

Slowly Elizabeth raised her head and opened her tear-filled eyes.

"I will return," he whispered. "I promise."

"You don't know that."

Guy sighed. "The other day, before Ruby and I headed to Owen's, I promised you we'd be apart for only a few hours. Liz, I make you that same promise again. You have my word."

Elizabeth stared at her husband.

"I know you think I've misled you and even lied to you these last few months. And I know you haven't completely forgiven me, but you must let me go. You must trust me."

Elizabeth placed a hand against Guy's face. "I trust you, Guy Payne."

Guy smiled. "I'm going to take the old dinghy we used to borrow. I'm sure it's still at the harbor."

"But it only fits two adults," Elizabeth noted.

"It's going to have to fit three for a little while," said Guy, "once I rescue Josiah and Happy." He kissed her on the forehead. "That's another reason I have to go alone."

"I reckon there ain't nothing we can say to get you to change that made-up mind of yours, is there?" Woody asked.

"I'm afraid not," Guy replied. He looked at the Rough Riders again. "I know you want to come, and I know the role of a soldier, but this battle I must fight alone." He gazed at Griffith, Ruby, and Graham. "I will meet you back at the house."

Then Guy headed off.

"Let's gather our belongings from the bench," Elizabeth said as her husband disappeared into the crowd. "Once the cranks leave, we'll go home and wait for Guy."

"I'll check the outfield for any stray baseballs," Griffith volunteered.

Yet in reality, he had something far different in mind.

• • •

As soon as the others headed for the dugout, Griffith started for the outer garden. But the moment he saw that everyone had their backs to him, he slipped off the green oasis and went to follow his father.

He spotted him right away, moving quickly through the crowd. At a couple of points, Guy walked on top of the bleachers like George had when he'd hurried down to the field. However, Griffith had to remain in the walkways. If he hopped onto the bleachers like his father, he risked being spotted by the Rough Riders. He knew it was only a matter of seconds until they discovered he was missing, and he couldn't chance being seen. He *needed* to go after his father. He couldn't let him go alone.

Once Griffith got out of the stadium, the crowd thinned considerably, though there were still plenty of people milling about. Guy crossed Barclay Street, and keeping a safe distance, Griffith followed. Passing horse-drawn carriages parked along the curb, where cranks were queued up and waiting for rides, Guy broke into a light jog. He crossed Guilford Street and then Calvert. Breathing heavily, Griffith wondered how much farther his father planned on traveling by foot. At some point would his father try to cut one of the carriage lines? They were losing precious time. At the very least, the Chancellor and his men were only several minutes ahead; at worst, they could already be at the boat launch.

Right before the corner of St. Paul Street, Guy slipped around a building and turned into a small alleyway. Griffith raced to the end of the building and peered down the narrow lane. Halfway down the block, his father had found an empty horse-drawn wagon. At the moment, he was standing beside it, talking with two men. Seconds

later, the three men climbed onto the front
seat. The wagon then headed up the alley in
Griffith's direction.

Griffith would have to board the moving
wagon. Ducking into a doorway so his father
wouldn't see him as they approached, he
held his breath. He'd jumped onto a moving
train before; how much more difficult could
this be?

"You can do this," he whispered to himself.

As the wagon neared, Griffith realized
his best chance to climb on was going to be
right after it turned the corner onto St. Paul
Street. But he had no idea what was in the
back. Was it empty or full? Would there be
anything to hide under?

Griffith watched the wagon make the turn.
Except for a few crates lining one side, the
back was entirely empty. Racing up behind
the wagon, which was already beginning to

pick up speed, Griffith knew he would have to scramble quickly to the front to avoid being seen.

Using some of the skills he'd learned from Woody way back in Minneapolis, Griffith grabbed hold of the thick chain clamped to the end of the open-backed wagon and hoisted himself aboard. Then, like a soldier snaking across the jungle floor, he squirmed on his belly over the uneven and ragged wooden planks to the front of the wagon.

He'd made it!

Curled in a ball against the back of the seat in which the three adults sat, Griffith's mind raced. How long was the ride to the harbor? What was happening to Josiah and Happy? Once they reached the pier, did his father really know where to go? He shut his eyes tightly and tried to listen to the conversation up front, but he wasn't able to hear it. The wagon seemed to stop at every corner. Where were they? He wanted to raise his head to peek out, but he didn't dare risk it.

He clutched his stomach. With each stop and lurch, the churning in his abdomen grew more intense, and when the wagon traveled over cobblestoned stretches, Griffith had to cover his mouth. The bumpy ride was far worse than any of the jolts and lurches he'd experienced on the many train trips this summer.

Griffith tried to focus on his father. In a few minutes he would have to confront him. What would he say? Should he do it right away? Griffith was so queasy he didn't know if he'd be able to speak once they stopped. Should he wait until they reached the dinghy?

But Griffith didn't get to make any of those decisions.

"Looks like we have ourselves a stowaway," one of the men said as the wagon slowed to a halt at the wharf.

Griffith didn't move. He remained in his fetal ball.

A hand shook his shoulder. "Let's go, young fella," said the other man.

Griffith sat up. His eyes met his father's.

"Griff!" Guy shouted. "What are you doing?"

Too nauseous to form words, Griffith didn't answer. He gripped the front of the wagon for balance, unable to tell what was spinning faster, his head or stomach.

"What are you doing?" Guy repeated. He helped his son from the wagon and propped him against one of the large rear wheels. "Do the others know you're here?"

Griffith's silence was his response.

"Oh, Griff." Guy felt his frown. "How could you do that to everyone?"

Still reeling, Griffith squeezed his brow. "I couldn't—I couldn't let you go alone."

"I *am* going alone," Guy said sternly.

Griffith started to shake his head, but his dizziness wouldn't allow it. "No way," he said softly. "I lost you once. I'm not losing you again. *We're* not losing you again."

"You won't, but this is too risky. I can't let—"

"No way," Griffith repeated, slowly regaining his balance. He motioned to the small boat tied to the pier. "I can fit in there with you."

Guy shook his head.

"Listen, Dad," said Griffith, able to stand on his own again. "I've been the man of our family this entire summer. I've looked out for Grammy, Ruby, and Mom everywhere we've gone. That's been my job, and it's still my job. I can't let you go alone. I have to do what's in the best interest of our family." Griffith

"I couldn't let you go alone."

placed a hand on his father's shoulder. "Your going alone is *not* in our best interest."

Guy stared at his son but didn't say a word.

"You need to let me, Dad. You have to let me help save Happy and Josiah, and you have to let me keep you safe. We need to work together."

Peering into his father's eyes, Griffith felt as if he was looking through an open window into Guy Payne's heart and mind. For the first time, he understood how it was for Ruby when she was able to see his thoughts in his face. His father recognized how much he'd matured. He was proud of his son. But at the same time, his father was riddled with guilt. He agonized over how much pain he'd caused his family. He dreaded causing them any more hurt.

"Be together," Guy whispered. "Always."

Griffith smiled his serious smile. "Always," he repeated.

"You make quite a strong case," Guy said. He clenched his fist and gently jabbed— love-tapped—Griffith's cheek.

Griffith pointed to the pier. "Let's go get our men and put an end to this war."

19

★

War on the Water

"**eep looking!" Guy urged.**

"I can't see a thing," Griffith said.

Night had fallen quickly, and although the fireworks from the celebration at Fort McHenry illuminated the sky from time to time, it was never for long enough.

Battling the salt water's sting, Griffith blinked hard and looked back at his father. Every muscle in Guy Payne's arms and shoulders bulged as he rowed the tiny vessel. His

"Keep looking!"

anguished expression pleaded for the small craft to move faster.

"They could be anywhere," said Griffith, searching the darkness.

"I know they're around here somewhere," Guy said, grimacing as he dragged the oars through the choppy waters. "They have to be. Just keep looking."

Upon leaving the pier, Guy had assured Griffith he knew exactly where they needed to go, but with each passing minute, Griffith wasn't so sure. Not only did his father's face contain fatigue and strain, but it was also holding more and more uncertainty.

"Trust your instincts, Dad," Griffith told his father, sensing his growing doubt. "Not once did your men ever lose faith in you. Don't lose faith in yourself."

"I won't," Guy grunted. "I promise." Then, as he continued to paddle and search, he began to speak to Griffith in a way he never had before. "I'm afraid he's going to murder them, Griff." His voice was somber. It also contained a trace of anger. "He's lost control. I'm afraid of what he may do."

Griffith didn't respond. Not even a nod. He was almost too stunned by his father's words to remember to scour the darkness.

"Griff, I know firsthand his preferred method of killing," Guy spoke to the waters. "I saw it. He drowns his victims."

Griffith winced.

"I watched him make an example of one of his men," Guy went on, "one who didn't follow his orders exactly as he wanted. He made me watch. Made the others witness it too. The man begged for his life, but the Chancellor did nothing. Just stood by as he struggled to stay afloat. But he couldn't swim, and his heavy suit and heavier boots pulled him under." Guy took several breaths. "You'd think it'd be easier to shoot someone, but with water, there are no bullets. It looks like a drowning, an accident. There's no evidence of wrongdoing, no suspicion of foul play, and chances are a body won't be found until much later, if they—"

"Look!" Griffith shouted.

He pointed skyward. Amid the darkness, he'd spotted the eagle. Soaring in from behind, the great bird swooped down over their craft and then banked upward to the east.

"He's telling us which direction to go!" Griffith exclaimed.

"But that's away from where we need to be," said Guy, propelling the oars as hard as he could. "Not far away, but . . . Griff, are you certain?"

"Yes, Dad," Griffith replied. "Absolutely certain."

Twice more the eagle dove down, circled the dinghy, and then glided off to the east. By the time the bird had started his second pass, Guy had already changed course.

As the waters splashed against the craft and lapped over the sides, Griffith climbed to the edge of the bow. In the distance he heard voices. Several different ones. He couldn't see where they were coming from or whom they belonged to, but they were getting louder and clearer.

"Think about what you're doing. Please don't do this. It's not too late."

"That's Josiah," Griffith whispered. "I'd recognize his voice anywhere."

Guy stopped rowing. He motioned for his son to remain silent and still.

"It's never too late. With breath, there's always hope. Please."

Guy leaned forward and tapped Griffith on the leg. He pointed to the waters off the starboard side. The outline of another vessel began to take shape. So did the silhouettes of several men.

"The Chancellor's right next to him," Guy

whispered, paddling the dinghy closer.

"Where's Happy?" asked Griffith, trembling. In a minute they'd be discovered. "I don't see him."

"It's never too late. You can—"

"Silence!" The Chancellor's voice. "Dispose of this man!"

Griffith and Guy were now only several boat lengths away, close enough to see what was taking place.

"Stop!" Guy called.

The Chancellor motioned to his men standing before him. Two held Josiah. Two others held Happy. All four had weapons. Would they use them?

"Don't do it!" shouted Guy.

"Look who's returned!" the Chancellor said, laughing. "Back for more, Mr. Payne?"

"Don't do it," Guy called again.

The Chancellor stepped to the edge of his boat and glared. Then he lifted the baseball from his pocket and rotated it in front of his face.

"Dispose of him now!" he ordered, while still staring down Guy. The crafts had drifted so close that the two men were only yards apart.

"No!" Griffith yelled.

"I may not have the boy *yet*," the Chancellor shouted, "but I have this." He raised the baseball over his head and shook it violently. "I will succeed. I will seize my true destiny."

Suddenly the Chancellor spun around, lowered his shoulder, and plowed into Happy. The two thugs let go of the old-timer, and he toppled overboard into the waters on the far side of the boat.

"No!" Guy screamed. He whirled to Griffith. "Row!" His voice exploded. "Fast!"

Leaning over the edge, Griffith frantically paddled with his arms, while his father plowed the oars through the waters. Listening to Happy's panicked cries and frenzied splashing, Griffith realized he'd only be able to bob his head in the rough surf a handful of times before going under.

"Paddle faster!" Guy shouted.

"I'm trying, Dad," yelled Griffith.

Now the Chancellor reached for Josiah, ripped him from the grasp of his men, and pulled him to the back of the boat.

"Almost there, Happy!" Guy called.

Griffith fought his tears. He knew it was only a matter of time before Josiah was in the water too. The Chancellor would be sure to dump Josiah overboard on the opposite side, making it impossible to rescue both men.

"This was meant for me." The Chancellor shook the baseball in front of Josiah's face. "You denied me my future. You chose another over me." His venomous voice grew louder. "This baseball would've worked for me, but you gave up on me. What kind of father gives up on his own son? What kind of—"

Whack!

For the first time in his life, Josiah struck his son, smacking his hollowed cheek.

But at the exact moment his fist met flesh, something else occurred. Josiah had raised his hand as he would when signaling the eagle. Out of nowhere, the great bird swooped down and jostled the Chancellor from behind. Josiah fell to the floor of the boat, while the baseball popped out of the Chancellor's hand.

It flew through the air—almost in slow motion—toward where Happy had been struggling in the water. However, the old-timer was now entirely submerged.

Without thinking, Griffith scrambled to his feet and hopped to the edge of the din-ghy, which rocked unsteadily. Then, just as Truman had leaped for the ball as it flew off the train, Griffith lunged for the baseball. Fully extended, he appeared to fly. Grabbing hold of a single, dangling thread with the tips of his fingers, he snared the ball before splashing down in the spot where Happy had gone under.

"Griff!" Guy called. "Hang on!"

"I got you!" Griffith shouted.

Upon hitting the water, Griffith felt Happy beneath the surface. He instantly hooked his arm under the old-timer's shoulder and somehow managed to hoist him upward.

But as soon as Happy broke the surface, he panicked.

"No!" Griffith screamed, before he was submerged. Surfacing and coughing up seawater, he tried to wrap his free arm around Happy, who violently flailed his limbs. "You're safe!"

But the Rough Rider couldn't calm down, and even though Griffith was a strong swimmer, Happy was pulling him under.

"I got—I got you!" yelled Griffith, his face inches from Happy's. "You're safe. Stop struggling!"

However, like any nonswimmer who believed he was drowning, Happy couldn't stop fighting.

"Put your arms—put your arms around my neck," Griffith said, dodging elbows. He desperately needed to steady the old-timer from behind. "Don't pull me—"

"Alexander Ethan Hoover!"

Guy's voice boomed. In all of his life, Griffith had never heard so loud a shout come from his father.

In an instant Happy's struggling ceased. The sound of his name—his *full* name— bellowed in the night had jolted him out of his panic.

Holding Happy afloat and still clutching the baseball, Griffith whirled onto his back and towed the old-timer toward the dinghy, which was now only feet away. Guy reached into the water. Using the little strength he hadn't expended and laboring to keep the boat from capsizing, he began lifting Happy onto the dinghy.

"Give me back my ball!" the Chancellor roared.

Leaning over the edge of his craft, the Chancellor fixed a demonic stare on the object in Griffith's left hand. With a rapid wave of the arm, he ordered his men to steer the boat toward the boy in the water.

"Hurry, Dad!" Griffith urged while shoving Happy's leg over the side. He peeked over his shoulder. The Chancellor was closing fast. "Hurry!"

"Push harder, Griff!" Guy pleaded.

Griffith reached under the water and, with one arm, lifted Happy toward the boat and hoisted his torso over the edge.

"Got him!" shouted Guy, grabbing the old-timer by the belt loop and pulling him all the way aboard.

But now the Chancellor was just a few feet from Griffith. With one of his thugs holding on to the suspenders under his coat, he reached as far as he could over the edge of his boat.

"Give it to me, Griffith Payne!"

Griffith gripped the edge of the dinghy. He wouldn't be able to pull himself on while still holding the baseball, and as water poured over all four sides, he didn't know if the vessel would stay afloat once he was aboard.

"Give me your hand!" Guy said, stepping around Happy. The dinghy rocked as he reached for his son.

At that moment the Chancellor lost his balance. Did he slip on the wetness? Did the rough surf knock him over? Did the man holding him let go?

Splash!

"I got you, Griff!" Guy called, clasping

his son's hand, the one without the baseball. "Hang on!"

Guy pulled his son with all his might, but the Chancellor had latched onto Griffith's foot and was swiping for the baseball. Once again Griffith was fighting to keep his head above water.

"Give it to me!" The Chancellor yanked on Griffith's foot and clawed at his other ankle.

Griffith swung his free leg away from the Chancellor. He couldn't allow him to grab hold. If he did, his father, whose grip on Griffith's hand was beginning to loosen, wouldn't be able to hang on.

"Griff!" yelled Guy, feeling his son slipping from his grasp.

Raising his free leg out of the water, Griffith whirled to the side. Then, with every ounce of strength he had left, he slammed his boot into the Chancellor's face.

Griffith was free.

"No!" the Chancellor shouted, still holding

Griffith's boot and flailing in the water. "No!"

In one motion, Guy leaned over the rocking dinghy, grabbed his son by the back of his trousers, and flipped him into the tiny craft. Gasping for air, Griffith landed beside Happy, still lying across the bottom of the boat, which was taking on more water by the second. Griffith sat up and hugged his father. Then he spotted the Chancellor, struggling to stay afloat. Like Happy moments ago, the Chancellor was panicking. He'd been so obsessed with the baseball, he'd allowed himself to fall into the water, even though he couldn't swim.

"Hold on, son!" Josiah called.

On the other boat, the Chancellor's men had moved aside as Josiah rushed to the edge. He knelt down and leaned out.

"I'm coming, son!" shouted Josiah. "Hold on!"

Peering through the darkness at Josiah, Griffith stared at his different-colored eyes.

The fireworks in the distant sky turned them red and blue. Each was filled with fear and dread and sorrow and pain.

"Don't leave me," Josiah said. "Please forgive me. I'm so sorry for all that—Don't leave me, George."

George.

Griffith cocked his head. George. The Chancellor's true identity.

Josiah reached for his hand.

George grabbed on.

"Don't leave me, George. I'm so sorry. We can—"

Then George let go. He stopped struggling, too. He simply looked at his father, nodded once, shut his eyes, and allowed himself to disappear underwater.

"George!" Josiah shouted. "George!"

Silence. The fireworks ceased. The desperate cries stopped. The only sound remaining on the bay was the lapping of water against the sides of the crafts.

He . . . allowed himself to disappear underwater.

Consumed by sadness, Josiah slumped forward and gazed across at Griffith. Amazingly, he managed a soft smile. As devastated as he was, Josiah understood that his child had finally found peace, a peace he'd been searching for all his life, though not the one Josiah had hoped he'd find.

Behind Josiah, the four dark-suited men stood confused. For the first time in ages, no one was there to tell them what to do.

Then, one by one, the four men removed the pink pocket squares from their jacket pockets and tossed them into the water.

As the boats drifted closer, Guy reached across with an oar and held it out to Josiah. But before the old man could grab it, two of the dark-suited men did and pulled the two crafts together. A third man retrieved a rope, while the fourth cleared space on deck so that everyone would be able to fit.

Once all were safely aboard the larger

vessel, Griffith and Guy sat down in front of Josiah. The old man didn't look up. His body heaved, his shoulders bounced. Clearly he was sobbing. Finally he raised his head.

"Your eyes," Griffith whispered. "They're—"

"Yes, Mr. Griffith." Josiah nodded.

His eyes were no longer different colors.

"I can see clearly now," Josiah whispered, leaking tears. "I understand all that I have done. I have insight."

Griffith stared into Josiah's new eyes. Something about them looked familiar, and it took only a moment for Griffith to realize what. Even through the darkness, Griffith could see they were a clear blue, the same eyes as the Chancellor's. Except the steely harshness had been replaced by a soft kindness.

Josiah smiled. "Yes, Mr. Griffith. I have my George's eyes now."

Griffith lowered his head. He stared at his cupped hands. They still held the baseball. He'd forgotten he was holding it.

Turning to his father, Griffith placed the baseball into Guy Payne's rugged hand, wrapped his fingers around it, and gently squeezed.

20

The Return

tanding in a line along the pier, the barnstormers searched the waters. Doc and the Professor held lanterns, Woody and Scribe peered through borrowed telescopes, Elizabeth clung to Ruby, and Preacher Wil knelt beside Truman.

After realizing that Griffith had set out after his father, the team opted to head to the harbor instead of back to the Paynes' house. Upon reaching the wharf, the dockworkers had confirmed what George had told them at Union Park: The Chancellor and his men had taken Josiah and Happy out into the harbor.

Graham stood at the end of the dock. They'd been waiting like this for nearly an hour, and there was still no sign of anyone. Barely a word had been spoken; all were too frightened to speak.

The barnstormers were angry as well. How could Griffith have run off like this? After what Ruby had put them through in Chicago, he knew the effect his disappearance would have on everyone. Heading downtown, the Professor had tried to assure the group that things would be okay, but of course, he had no way of knowing. At one point, Woody snapped at the Professor and told him—

Graham leaned out. In the distance, two dots—one large, one small—appeared on the water. He tried to identify the shapes: two vessels, tethered together. He glanced down the row. The others saw it too. Like Graham, they'd all stepped to the edge of the pier.

As the boats neared, the rhythmic sound of the two crafts knocking against each other and the rattle of chains keeping time with the tide grew louder. Squinting, Graham could see people. Everyone was standing on the large boat; the dinghy was empty.

Graham saw his older brother first. A wave of relief rushed through his limbs. He spotted Josiah's distinctive shape next. Then Happy. Followed by his father. For the first time since Union Park, Graham could breathe again.

The Chancellor's men were also on the boat. Two stood in the front, two others in the back. All four were rowing, steering the boat ashore.

But there was no sign of the Chancellor.

Slowly the faces and forms came into clearer view. They all wore solemn expressions, as if they were returning from battle.

Which they were.

Graham was the first one to greet the boats. Standing at the end of the dock, he reached for his father's hand.

Guy Payne passed the baseball to his son.

21

★

Farewell to Friends

amden Station was bustling on Friday morning. Workers were heading to their jobs, and families were leaving on trips, looking to get an early start on the last weekend of summer.

The barnstormers were gathered at the depot too. The Rough Riders would be departing today. Some of their trains left in the morning, others in the afternoon. By evening they'd all be off, going their separate ways.

By evening they'd all be off.

Of course, the Paynes accompanied the soldiers to the station, vowing to remain until the last veteran left.

"We're going to be the bridge," Guy said to the group assembled on the platform. He had his arm around his wife's waist. "We're going to make sure we all stay connected."

"I'll personally see to it that we have annual reunions," Elizabeth added. "I want you to remain in our lives, and our children need you to be a part of theirs. We're one big extended family now."

Josiah was the only one not at the station. He'd gone to a lawyer's office at first light because he wanted to resolve his son's estate matters as quickly as possible. He also didn't want to bid farewell to the Rough Riders. After yesterday, he wasn't in any condition for good-byes. Still, he'd promised to stop by the Paynes' home later in the week before he headed off.

"All aboard!"

A conductor stood at the end of the platform. He waved a clipboard and pointed passengers to the first car of the train waiting in the station.

The barnstormers faced Happy. "Back to New Orleans," he announced, tipping his cap to his teammates.

"Where are your belongings?" Elizabeth asked.

"Everything I need is right here with me." He motioned to his person. "I gave my satchel to Josiah, a gift for his kindness and generosity of spirit." He stepped toward the track and patted the side of the train. "As soon as I find my seat, I believe I'm going to sleep until I reach the Crescent City. Then once I'm home, I'm going to sleep some more." He laughed. "Then I'll probably sleep some more before figuring out what I'm going to do with that house and the rest of my days."

Shortly after Happy's train left the station, the one for Bubbles, Doc, and Woody pulled in. The three would be heading west together, though they weren't all going to the same place.

Bubbles was meeting his wife and eleven kids near Cincinnati. Then they were all off to Dayton to help their relatives with their flying contraption. But at this point, Bubbles didn't even know if Wilbur and Orville were still working on it.

Doc was heading to Ohio too. He was raised in Texas, but he'd spent most of his adult life just outside of Cleveland. He was thinking about returning to school so he could become a surgeon. "Time to live up to my nickname," he proclaimed.

Woody was going home to start a family. He'd spent too many years in the factories, and after what he'd lived through these last two summers, he now realized what was most important to him.

"I reckon it's time for me to stop puttin'

off what the wifey's been askin' for since before McKinley was elected president," he announced.

Then Woody pulled Griffith aside.

"When we headed out on this adventure a month ago," he said, placing both hands on Griffith's shoulders, "I sat beside a boy on that train ride to Cincinnati." Woody nodded and smiled. "As we head our separate ways in search of new adventures, I reckon I stand before a man. A good man."

"Take—" Griffith started to speak, but stopped. He couldn't trust his voice to say the desired words. He swallowed hard as Bubbles, Doc, and Woody walked away.

Scribe, Tales, and the Professor were scheduled to leave on the next train, a train that originated in Boston and had a final destination of San Francisco, California (with scores of stops along the route). However, it didn't leave until after lunch. Hence, the

Paynes were able to enjoy one last meal with the remaining Rough Riders. They picnicked by the harbor, near where they'd distributed the fliers earlier in the week. The group told Guy about the come-from-behind win in the River City, the slugfest in Chicagoland, and the triumphs in the Crescent City, interrupting and ribbing one another throughout.

As soon as they finished eating, the trio had to leave.

Scribe would probably get off near his hometown of Oklahoma City, but the mountain of a man hadn't yet made up his mind exactly where he was heading. "I'll go quietly," he said. "I'll figure out where I'm going when I get there."

Unlike Scribe, Tales knew exactly where he was going. The second sack man was returning to his friends and family in the Louisville area.

"I'm looking for a new adventure," the

Professor said. "Never seen the Pacific Ocean. I think it's about time I do."

After the threesome departed, only one member of the Travelin' Nine remained, Preacher Wil. His train didn't leave for another hour, but after saying good-bye to all the others, he wasn't much for socializing and preferred to be alone. He spent most of that hour sitting on a bench near the entrance to the station. Truman was with him, lying across his boots.

A few minutes before his train was slated to arrive, Preacher Wil joined the Paynes on the platform. As he approached, Griffith, Ruby, and Graham all noticed his stoic expression.

"What is it?" Griffith asked.

"Is something the matter?" added Ruby.

"Truman and I had a long talk this afternoon," Preacher Wil said.

The hound sat down in front of Graham and stared up at the youngest Payne.

"What did you two discuss?" Graham asked, chuckling. He peered down at the dog and pretended to tap his foot impatiently. "I'm waiting, Truman. Tell me about this conversation."

"Listen closely, Graham," said Preacher Wil. "He's speaking to you right now."

"I can hear him," Griffith said, smiling. He knelt down to Truman and began scratching behind his ears. Then he looked up at Preacher Wil. "He wants to stay," he said.

Preacher Wil nodded.

"No," Elizabeth said, shaking her head. "Truman is your companion. He stays with you."

"It is something we both discussed." Preacher Wil pointed to Truman. "This is an old hound. He is a loyal companion, but he is also tired. The travel has taken a toll."

"But you'll be alone," Ruby said, kneeling next to Truman.

"I can never be alone." Preacher Wil reached under his collar and twirled his charm. "I'm sure I'll find myself another canine companion. Maybe not as special as this old hound, but one who'll keep me company. Don't you worry."

"Are you sure?" asked Ruby, staring into Truman's eyes.

Graham squeezed his baseball with both hands and looked at his father. "I always wanted a dog. I've been hounding you for one for years." He laughed. "Get it? *Hounding* you?"

"We get it, Grams," Ruby said, rolling her eyes.

"At this juncture in his walk," Preacher Wil explained, "he prefers a roof over his head and a yard to play in. You can provide him with that. He's chosen you as much as you want him." He pivoted to Ruby. "I've known this day would come since we first met in Jackson Park. The moment I laid eyes on you I knew something had changed." Preacher Wil turned to Griffith. "Then he took to you like I've never seen him take to anyone but me. He wouldn't leave your side. He did everything in his power to protect you, all three of you." Preacher Wil sighed. "He told you his name. Truman. He chose to tell you that." He sighed again. "My journey is about to resume. My journey, my walk. He belongs with you."

"Preacher Wil," said Elizabeth, "if you ever change your mind, he's yours."

Preacher Wil smiled, a tinge of wistfulness tugging at the corners of his mouth. "He is all of ours. He belongs with you, but Truman will live inside each one of us forever." He clasped his hands over his chest. "May God help us be everything Truman believes that we are."

With those words, Preacher Wil headed down the platform toward his train. Griffith,

Ruby, Graham, Elizabeth, and Guy all realized they would probably never see him
again. Even though Guy and Elizabeth had
promised to bring the Travelin' Nine together
again, they sensed Preacher Wil wouldn't be
present at those gatherings.

When the Paynes exited Camden Station,
they were greeted by one more surprise.
Josiah had returned. He stood on the far side
of Howard Street. They hurried across.

"What are you doing here?" asked Ruby.

"We thought we weren't going to see you
until tomorrow at the earliest," Guy added.

"I finished up quickly with the lawyers,
Mr. Guy," Josiah explained. "Very quickly,
in fact. I've been here since the morning,
watching and waiting from just up the
block." He waved to the buildings beyond
the entrance to the terminal. "I didn't say
good-bye this morning because I didn't
know if I'd be able to muster the strength.

When I finished early, I came straight here, but I couldn't . . . Once I arrived, I still couldn't get myself to bid these great gentlemen farewell."

Guy rested his hand on the old man's shoulder. "What did the attorneys tell you?"

"I was quite surprised, Mr. Guy." Josiah pushed his wire-framed glasses up the bridge of his nose. "My son died intestate."

Guy flinched. "He didn't have a will?" He reached for Elizabeth's hand.

"Perhaps my son believed he was invincible. He'd become quite delusional." Josiah shrugged. "Or maybe he thought it was bad luck to have a will. Or it could've been something he just hadn't gotten around to taking care of." He stared at Guy with his clear blue eyes. "No matter how you look at it, Mr. Guy, it was a careless lapse in judgment for a man of such power and wealth."

"So what happens to all his money?"

Graham asked. He'd sat down cross-legged on the asphalt next to Truman, and the hound had placed his snoot on Graham's thigh.

"What about everything he owns?" Griffith tilted his head.

Josiah smiled, and for a brief instant, Griffith thought he saw Josiah's eyes flicker back to their different colors.

"Why are you smiling?" Ruby asked.

"Money, property, possessions—it all belongs to his next of kin, Miss Ruby," Josiah answered. "That would be me."

"You get everything?" Graham's eyes bulged.

"Indeed, Mr. Graham," Josiah replied. "All his assets and all his debts, too." He looked to Elizabeth and Guy. "Including the debt you allegedly owe."

"What does that mean?" Ruby wondered, joining Graham on the pavement next to Truman.

"It means, Miss Ruby, I have the power to absolve the Payne family of its debt."

"Absolve?" asked Graham.

"Forgive," Josiah replied. "Rid your family of this burden." He stepped forward to place his hand against the side of Ruby's head. "And I do." Turning to Guy, he reached into the satchel that Happy had given him, and pulled out a large envelope. He handed it to Guy.

"We no longer owe the money?" Elizabeth asked. She peered over her husband's shoulder as he opened the letter.

"Owe?" Josiah laughed. "All of my son's money and possessions now belong to the Payne family."

"Oh, no," said Guy adamantly. He stuffed the letter back in the envelope and held it out to Josiah. "We could never take such a gift. Put it to much better use than simply giving—"

"I can think of no better use, Mr. Guy," Josiah cut him off.

"I think you already have," Guy countered, staring at the old man. "I would much prefer if you used it for *that*."

Josiah sighed. He looked down at Truman, and when he did, the hound hopped to his feet. He hobbled next to Josiah, brushing up against his leg.

"Whatever remains," Guy added, "we will divide equitably among our family. Among the barnstormers."

Griffith looked from his father to Josiah and then back at his father. He didn't understand what they were talking about. He glanced at his siblings and then at his mother. They appeared to be just as perplexed.

For what felt like minutes but was surely only seconds, Guy and Josiah stared at each other.

Finally the old man spoke.

"Yes, Mr. Guy," he whispered. "I will go along with this plan."

Guy nodded and then turned to his wife. "Liz, would it be all right with you if we have a houseguest for a while?"

"It would be my pleasure."

"You're coming to live with us?" Graham leaped to his feet, holding his baseball to his chest.

"Yes, Mr. Graham," Josiah replied, ruffling the youngest Payne's hair. "That's the plan. But first I will need to go to the mountains to get my affairs in order, not that I have many." He pointed to the eagle perched high atop a church steeple beyond Camden Station. "And he needs to go home. Then I will return."

"The plan?" asked Griffith, once again alternating his eyes between Josiah and his father. "What plan?"

"May I?" Guy asked Josiah.

"Please do, Mr. Guy," Josiah replied, his eyes twinkling. "Tell them your plan."

"We are going to help the Chancellor's men," he said. "We are going to change their evil ways and rehabilitate them as best we can. Using the money, we'll help those who worked for him in every way possible, so long as they promise to become law-abiding citizens. We'll dismantle what the Chancellor has built, undo what he has done. We will achieve all this through baseball. We'll establish a whole new league."

"I know what we can call it," Griffith added, raising a fist. "The American League!"

22

★

The Magic Baseball

Before we go home," Graham said, "can we make one final stop?"

"Where would you like to go?" asked Elizabeth.

"Back to the harbor. I want to see if I can find George. To tell him thanks and say good-bye."

Guy smiled. "I think that can be arranged," he said.

The Paynes had waited for Josiah and the eagle to disappear up St. Paul Street before beginning their final journey of the summer. They were less than a block into it when Graham made his request.

As they walked toward the wharf, they no longer looked over their shoulders. Nor did they pay attention to faces in the crowd or concern themselves with sudden noises or odd activities. They no longer had to.

Graham led his family onto the street where the boys had been playing ball the other day. At first he wasn't certain they'd turned down the correct block, since all the side streets—with the tall brick buildings, sagging clotheslines, open windows, and foul odor—looked identical. However, as soon as he saw the baseball lines drawn in chalk on the pavement, he knew they were in the right place.

Then he spotted the boys. They weren't in the middle of a game. Rather, they were sitting on a stoop midway up the block. Of

course George was there, his grin extending from cheek to chubby cheek. He popped
up like a spring the moment he saw his new
friend.

"Hey, Graham." George jumped off the
top step onto the sidewalk.

"How's it going, George?"

"Going great!" George picked up a mitt
from the sidewalk, put it on, and pounded
it with a fist. "You here to play? We're getting ready to pick sides. You can play on my
team."

Graham shook his head. "Maybe some
other time." He removed the baseball from
his pocket. "We're heading home, but before
we left, I wanted to give you something."

Graham turned to his family. He hadn't
told them what he was planning to do, fearing they might object. But as he looked to
them now, Graham saw his worries weren't
necessary. He had their blessing.

"This is for you," Graham said.

He flipped the baseball into the air, and as it sailed toward George, a gentle breeze began to blow.

With two hands, George caught the baseball. "What am I supposed to do with it?" he asked, examining it. "It's falling apart. I can't play with this."

"Keep it anyway," Graham said. "I don't need it anymore, but I think you will."

"How?" asked George, scrunching his face into a Graham-like knot.

"You will. Trust me."

Raising the baseball to his face, George studied it more closely. He teased the loose stitching and then placed his finger over the hole. George shuddered. Clearly he'd felt something. A shiver?

"You sure you don't want to play?" George asked, tucking the ball into a pocket.

Graham shook his head. "One more thing,

A gentle breeze began to blow.

George," he added, holding up a single finger. "See the things that others don't."

George scrunched his face into a knot again. "Am I supposed to know what that means?"

Graham laughed. He looked at his brother and sister. "He's such a babe."

"You will one day," Griffith answered George.

"If you say so," said George, rubbing his button nose. Then he removed the oversize cap from his head and placed it on Graham's. "This is for you."

Before Graham had the chance to say thank you, George was running out to his position in right garden.

"I hope he doesn't lose it," Griffith said.

"He won't," said Graham, speaking to the field. "He's going to put it to good use."

With all his heart, Graham was certain he'd done the right thing. George was going to love baseball more than anyone ever had, and he was going to cherish the attention and limelight.

Graham turned to his older brother. "George is going to take good care of baseball." He reached over and tapped Griffith's temple. "Some things you just know."

"You know what I know?" said Griffith as they started back down the street. "Everything we could ever need is right here."

As a family, Guy, Elizabeth, Griffith, Ruby, Graham, and Truman Payne rounded the corner and headed for home.

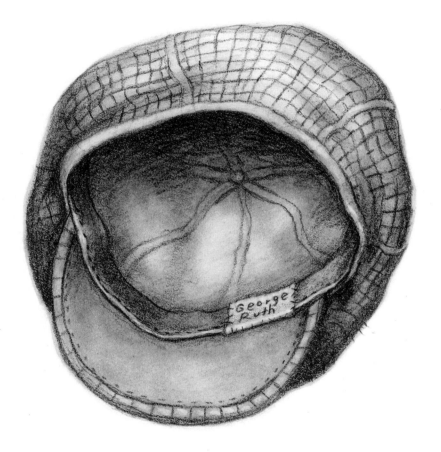